Mosaic
Anthology

By Monique DeMille

MOSAIC ANTHOLOGY
Copyright © 2020 by Monique DeMille

ISBN 978-1-7363175-1-8 (pbk)
ISBN 978-1-7363175-0-1 (ebook)

Published by Moxie Books

Front cover image by Canva Design
Editing by DML Editing & Writing

Printed in the United States of America

First Printing, 2020

Dedication

For those who doubted me, I forgive you…

For those who inspired me, I thank you…

And for those who had faith in me, I love you…

Enough is Enough

Used to think I wasn't

smart enough

good enough

woman enough

Used to think I wasn't

pretty enough

light skinned enough

shapely enough

Used to think I wasn't

brave enough

strong enough

tough enough

A voice whispered to my soul proclaiming

You are more than enough

Life at A Glance

Mama never told me there would be days like this. As I stood at the threshold of the church, my mind couldn't help but wander to the prior week trying to recall what it had missed. My body stood listless. Silence filled my ears and tried to hush my thoughts but to no avail. With my eyes a gazed and my fists clenched tight, my face began to swell with emotion. It was an intensity of emotion that I could not control even if someone had shown me how.

The last two weeks had been somewhat difficult for us, but never did I think it would come to this. Never could I have imagined what lie before me on this Saturday afternoon in the sweltering southern heat. I recall vividly waking up the other morning with Martin still asleep beside me. I rolled over, laid my head on his chest and tried to become one with his soul. I loved the way my head would rise and fall to the beat of his breaths. He was so precious to me and every moment we spent together was magical. When he would finally awaken, he would look at me with this grin that would warm me in places that only God could see. I often heard that in life a person gets one, maybe two true loves. Well, I was convinced I had found mine.

Martin was the sweetest man that I had ever known. I remember the night he proposed to me. We were on vacation in Hawaii enjoying dinner on the beach by candlelight. Shortly after we finished our entrees, the waiter brought us dessert and two glasses of champagne. However, my glass of champagne had some extra sparkle to it. Unbeknownst to me, Martin had asked the server to place the engagement ring in my glass before bringing it to the table. As the three violinists played, Martin got down on his bended knee and asked me to marry him. It was a moment that I would cherish forever.

The numbness of what was before me started to overcome my entire body. My mouth went dry, my throat grew a lump the size of a golf ball making it hard to swallow, and my legs grew heavier as time stood still. Stuck within the moment, I could not move. I could not turn away. I could not run. I could not even fall down. I could find no way to hide myself from the grief and despair that my mind and body had so quickly succumb to. All I could do was remain steadfast between the doors of the church helplessly in pain.

As a tear began to roll down my check, a woman sitting in the pew next to me reached out her hand.

Strangely, I did not even realize this woman had touched me because my eyes were pierced on the events unfolding at the front of the church while the rest of my body stood in awe, completely unaware of its surroundings. She was a kind and gentle older woman who was wearing a stylish lilac suit with a matching silk scarf and hat.

"Ma'am, there's room next to me right here if you want to sit down," she whispered.

The golf ball in my throat was growing even larger preventing me from responding. I kindly smiled and nodded my head as if I understood the words that were coming out of her mouth. I had lost track of time and was not even aware of how long she had tried to get my attention.

The church was decorated with flowers throughout. The pews were lined with glass tapered bud vases filled with Persian lilacs, white hydrangeas, lavender and white roses. From the ceiling, near the pulpit, hung large cascading floral arrangements, which were quite pleasing to the senses. A feeling of happiness filled the room, for most, as the pianist played angelic tunes. For a few others, such as me, the candlelight that filled the room illuminated the anger and resentment shown upon the faces of the audience. Unanswered questions soared through my head and hit me in the chest taking my breath away.

"Ma'am…pssst…pssst. I said there is room right here for you. I was saving this seat for my sister, but she must not be coming."

Slowly I turned my head to face the sweet voice that buzzed in my ear. "Thanks ma'am, but I won't be needing a seat as I ain't plannin' on staying long."

I could not formulate the words to tell her that my heart was crying inside and that even if I wanted to, I could not move my legs to walk any closer and take a seat beside her. The heat from outside was creeping up from behind. As it approached, it wrapped itself around my arms and legs. I tried to shake it off, but it was just as hot as my temperament. Beads of sweat began dripping from my forehead; mixing in with the tear drops that continued to stream down my face. Aside from the shock, I could also taste the saltiness of my sorrow upon my lips. My palms were drenched with sweat causing my purse handle to start sliding from my tight grip.

"What did I miss," I muttered to myself in anger.

"What in God's name did I miss?"

The angelic melodies stopped, and the congregation focused their attention upfront. The words spoken by the preacher were muddled and unclear. I felt like I was lost in translation of the words spewing from the preacher's mouth and unable to make sense of my surroundings. I could clearly see the preacher's lips moving but could not make out the sounds that escaped them. I could recall receiving a phone call from a close friend urging me to make my way to the church downtown. But I could not for the life of me envision the streets I took that led me there, or could I recall who I might have passed along the way. All I knew was that Martin was there and near him was where I had to be.

While the preacher continued chanting, the walls of the church closed in tighter leaving less air for me to breathe. Praying that my eyes were deceiving me, I looked further down the aisle. Past the people sitting on both sides of the church; past the decorated pews; past the clusters of candle lights; and past the group of people congregated on both sides of the alter – there he stood. Martin Lansing, the man that I adored, was standing at the alter but he wasn't alone. Faced towards him was a woman dressed in a long white gown with a veil upon her head.

"...I promise to love you until death do us part...," he uttered to the woman dressed in stark white as he placed a ring upon her finger.

"What? What did he just say?" I thought to myself. This must be a dream or a nightmare because I know this cannot be happening for real. I know that I am not standing here in the doorway of this church watching the man that I love with all my heart vow his love for someone else. This cannot be. I must be having some sort of out-of-body experience. "This simply cannot be," I mumbled as I tried to convince myself.

"...I now pronounce you man and wife.....," proclaimed the preacher.

Upon hearing those words my knees got weak. I decided to take the elderly woman up on her offer and accept the seat beside her. With my face in my hands I bowed my head and cried uncontrollably. The woman in the lilac suit did not know what to make of my outburst and did what, I think, came natural to her. She began slowly rubbing my back and assuring me that everything was going to be okay.

"Don't fret yourself," she said. "Don't fret yourself about it, dear."

By the time I raised my head and mustered up enough gumption to walk without feeling utterly ashamed, Martin and his new bride had exited the church. The congregation was quickly making their way outside with their small sacks of rice to congratulate the bride and groom. As I walked towards the church doors to join the commotion outside, I looked down at the engagement ring on my finger that Martin bought me two years ago.

I loved my ring. I loved Martin. I loved the love that we shared. As I continued making my way towards the doors to leave the church, I could not do anything but shake my head and wonder what went wrong between us. Just the other weekend him and I were at my condo hugged up watching movies, eating popcorn and laughing with our favorite comedians. Now, today the world is laughing at me. Laughing at how oblivious I must have been to reality. How careless I had been for not noticing that he was planning a future with someone else the whole time I was planning my future with him.

Outside the church the crowd enveloped the couple making it hard for me to reach them. I wanted badly to walk up to Martin, kiss the groom and slap the bride. I wanted to show the world that he really was mine and that he did not belong to this lady dressed in white, regardless of what the preacher had proclaimed earlier. As reality began sinking further into the trenches of my stomach, my knees became weaker. My life, as I knew it, had just come to an end while their life together was in full bloom. With this realism staring me in the face and a fragile heart, I fell to my knees.

All I could do was cry. I cried, and I cried, and I cried. I cried until no more tears could fall from my eyes. The man that I had cherished for the past three years was gone and things would never be the same.

The Dance

Imagine two people,

their souls so entangled with desire

that they dance as if they are one

and no one is watching…

So taken by the essence of the moment

that they are deafened to the echoes of lust

that cry from within the depths of their souls

yearning to be unleashed.

Imagine passion so intense

that it soars wildly, fiercely, uncontrollably

through the walls of their minds…

it scorches their flesh to the touch

and leaves them still wanting more…

To their *own* rhythm, they continue to dance…

Raven's Box

It's Monday night and the clock just flashed 9:23 p.m. He is five minutes late. Every Monday night at exactly 9:17 p.m. Raven and Jared meet in cyber space to exchange endless conversations filled with highlights of their daily routines and compelling thoughts of holding each other again. It has been almost a year since Jared accepted the position with an information technology company as an IT Director and moved to the east coast. And a few months since he last visited her in Chicago. And it had been one week since she was able to connect with him through her personal home computer. He made the decision to move to New Jersey without Raven's consent.

When he left last May, they agreed they would commit to meet every Monday night at exactly 9:17 p.m. This scheduled chat time was Raven's way of helping to keep their relationship vibrant and somewhat connected.

She figured that if he could commit to meeting her online once a week and break away from whatever he was doing, then he must really love her as he so proclaimed. So far, her theory had proved to be right. Since Jared moved to the east coast, they had only missed one Monday night and had been no more than ten minutes late meeting online.

Even if he had to work late, Jared would log on to his computer and tap into the life of his distant love. He loved to hear about her day at the office and all of the intriguing characters she worked alongside. It helped him feel connected to her everyday life and ease the pain of their distance. Although he seldom mentioned it, he longed to see her and wished she had decided to move to the east coast with him.

In the beginning, she did not know how she would handle him relocating without her. Jared possessed a distinctive and alluring trait that was only found in a few good men. The way he would gently stroke Raven's hair with his resilient, yet delicate touch was like a kiss on the small of the neck; sweet, innocent and endearing. The two of them had always been inseparable. They enjoyed each other's company and shared many of the same interests. They were both avid readers and could find the beauty in different cultures and people. Watching movies was also a favorite pastime of theirs. Friday nights were Raven's night to pick the movie and of course, Saturday selections were reserved for Jared. They watched everything from foreign to old classic to urban films.

Initially his acceptance of the position at a tech company was contingent upon Raven accepting his offer to move with him. She entertained the thought for about a week but then decided against it. She wanted to accept his invitation to join him on his quest to become successful and financially secure, but reality began staring her in the face. Jared loved her – she knew that unquestionably. He had proven that repeatedly. However, marriage was something that he avoided at all costs. He wanted a wife and family one day but just not right now, he often told her. To be honest, she was not keen on the idea of marriage either.

Although his career was headed in an upward direction Raven's was too and she did not feel they should hold each other back. Moving in with him would mean sacrificing her professional goals and aspirations, which she was not prepared to do. She was recently promoted to Marketing Director after years of hard work and stolen recognition. Torn between supporting the man she loved and pursuing her own dreams of success, Raven chose the latter. She could not bring herself to walk away from what she had worked so hard to attain. Consequently, she began to accept the fact that the time may never come for them to commit themselves unconditionally to one another and take each other's hand in marriage; especially if he was moving to the east coast.

They were both too selfish in nature. Until death do us part. The thought of those words often sent chills down her spine. Was that just something that was said for nostalgic sake or did she really have to mean those spoken words? That could mean forever and at the age of twenty-eight she was not ready for forever. She knew that she would forever be dedicated to her career and her own happiness but could not vow to be dedicated to Jared forever. Not now anyway, and maybe never.

She'd made many mistakes over the years. Like getting a tattoo with her fiancé's name on it, followed by an impromptu marriage at the age of nineteen that was annulled six months later. These were some of the stains of her past. The more she stared at her ankle, which still bore the name of her ex-husband, the less appealing the whole idea of another long-term commitment seemed. Besides, she felt that a life of marriage with kids and a big house with a white picket fence was highly overrated. It was a fallacy that she could wait a few more years to disprove.

"Where is he?" she mumbled to herself. The time was now 9:27 p.m. and still no sign of Jared. She was growing more impatient and anxious by the minute. She longed to hear the sound of the squeaky door opening which announced his arrival to their cyber space love chat.

"He must be out with another woman", she quickly thought, "and unable to break away for one lousy moment to spend some quality time with me. Why do I even waste my time with him?" She already knew the answer to that question.

When life had taken its toll on her sanity, the one true thing that she could depend on was the soothing conversation that only her man could bring. As she sat there sulking and waiting, she began clicking on various hyperlinks. One romance horoscope link carried her into a love-test site. From there she went to a for-women-only web site that took her to a lesbian chat room. From there she connected to a send-a-greeting-for-free site, and so on and so on. In the midst of clicking, reading and mapping over into forbidden zones she heard the sound of a screeching door opening ajar. He had arrived.

"Hey love. Sorry I'm late. I was hung up at work. I was hoping that I didn't miss you."

"No, I'm here. I'm always here for you. Since when did you start working so late? You're not having an office affair on me, are you?"

"No…no…Nothing like that. I'm just working on a new project and got held up."

"Okay, well I guess I forgive you."

"What are you wearing?"

"I have on the long black Victoria's Secret night gown that you bought me last Christmas. With no panties!!"

"Can I come over and take it off you?"

"Sure, but you better hurry up. My boyfriend is the jealous type and he will be home soon!"

"Oh, I'm sure he won't mind. You know it ain't no fun if your homies can't have none."

"Ha-Ha-Ha! Real funny Jared. If you keep that up neither you nor your homies will get any! Anyway…did you check on the flight prices? I'm dying to see you again."

"Yes, I did, love. It will cost you $297.00 round-trip," said Jared.

"Correction. You mean it will cost YOU $297.00 round-trip," said Raven.

"Whatever," exclaimed Jared.

"Oh, are you saying that you aren't going to buy my ticket to come see you? Have you found another woman to keep you warm at night," questioned Raven with a bit of jealously seething through her message?

"No, I'm not saying that at all. Baby, you know I'd do anything for you."

"Sure, you would. Tell me anything."

"Well, for your information, Ms. Raven, I already booked your flight and bought the ticket. It will be waiting for you at the ticket counter at O'Hare. Your flight leaves out next Monday at 6:25 a.m."

"You're kidding, right?"

"No, I'm not kidding. What…you've changed your mind…you're not coming?"

"Of course, I'm coming! I wouldn't dare miss a chance to see you!" Raven was barely able to hold back her excitement.

"Okay, well I'm going to let you go now. I did just get in and I'm pretty tired."

"I understand. Call me on Friday when you get off, okay?"

"Okay. I love you."

"I love you, too! Smooches!"

"Your man has left the room", said the pre-recorded voice on the computer. Followed by the sound of a rickety door slamming shut.

One week, she thought. She had only one week before she faced the man who she had only had the chance to chat with online for the last eight months. It had been brutal not seeing him, but this trip would make it all worth it.

It is time for a little me time, Raven thought. Every other night, right before bedtime, Raven performed a pampering ritual that her grandmother swore by. Her grandmother shared this ritual with her years ago. It was the secret to her youthful appearance. When her grandmother passed away, she was 82 years old, but she did not look a day over 45. Her youthful look was most certainly attributed to good genes but also good skincare habits. She always started with delicately cleansing her skin with an oatmeal scrub. Granny always said that a woman's skin was as delicate as a rose petal so be sure to rub it gently.

After cleansing the face, she would follow up with an egg and apricot mask. Once the mask dried, she gently removed it with cotton balls soaked in lemon juice. Next, she soaked her face in a bowl of ice water for exactly three minutes. Any longer than that would cause the pores to constrict too much and any less would cause them not to constrict enough. The last step was said to be critical in the process. This routine was the secret to her flawless caramel-colored skin tone and texture. She always received compliments on how beautiful and radiant her skin looked from strangers and friends. Her beauty was an irresistible lure to men.

Just as Raven was finishing her bedtime ritual, there was a knock at the front door. She raced to the window only to find a black Ford Explorer parked outside. Soulful sounds of music blared from within the truck. It was Cameron. Cameron was a longtime friend of Jared's. They grew up together on the streets of Detroit and engaged in everything from selling drugs in rural neighborhoods as youths to stealing candy from Middle Eastern owned corner stores near their homes.

Raven and Cameron met about seven years ago one night at a local dance club. She was out with her girlfriend,

Brandi, when a very appealing man approached her and asked her to buy him a drink.

"Buy you a drink? I don't think so," snapped Raven.

"Well, why not? Tonight is Ladies Night. You didn't pay to get in here so you should be able to afford to buy me a drink," the stranger replied.

"It's not a matter of what I can afford. It's a matter of what I am going to do. And what I am not going to do is buy you a drink," declared Raven.

"All right then fine. I'll buy you one. But only if I can pull up a chair and sit with you," said the stranger.

How could she refuse this obnoxious, sexy sculpture of a man who stood before her? His eyes fixated on her like that of a self-portrait hanging above the mantel of a fireplace. His smile welcomed her and grabbed her attention without asking permission. He was the true epitome of sex dressed in a black Italian suit. The fabric of his suit softly outlined his muscular physique giving just enough definition to his bodily tone. He might turn out to be Mr. Right for all she knew. Even though he appeared to be overly sure of himself, she could not refuse his abrupt invitation.

"Sure, you can buy me a drink and chat with me for a minute. But only if you promise not to sit too close. I don't want people thinking we're together when we're not," said Raven.

"Okay, that's fair. I'll be right back with your drink," he replied.

If only she would have declined his invitation for casual conversation that evening maybe she would not be in the predicament she was in now.

"Hello, Cameron. To what do I owe the pleasure of this visit tonight," questioned Raven.

"I just got off of work and needed to see your smiling face," he cunningly replied.

He was good at pouring on the charm and she was good at falling for it. As he stood in the threshold of her quaint townhouse, wearing a pair of black slacks and a camel sweater that hugged him in all of the right places, her body screamed, "Take me!" The thought of him thrusting inside her was almost too much to bear. The more she tried to separate herself from the sedative pleasures he brought her, the more she found herself wanting more. His genitals flirted with secluded places inside of her that shied away from others. If loving him was wrong, then why did it feel so right?

"Come on in. Ummm...I guess you couldn't call first, huh," she said.

"Thank you, babe. Why do I need to call? I know you're home. At least you had better be home at this time of night. Don't have me out here looking for you girl," he said jokingly. "You know I will drive up and downtown looking for my Boo."

As he passed by her, she could smell the lingering aroma of his spiced cologne. It teased her senses and invited her to come closer. She reached out her arms and he accepted her embrace with his touch.

"Mmmmm. It sure is good to see you, sexy. You're looking lovely as ever. Mmmm… damn you feel good," said Cameron.

Raven's hormones were soaring wildly. Moisture surged from within, as her mind anticipated what her body might be just moments away from experiencing. She took a deep breath and tried to focus on the conversation at hand and not the sculpture that stood before her calling out in a language only her body could understand.

"Thank you. You don't look so bad yourself,"
teased Raven.

"It's a shame that Jared still doesn't realize that he
left a good thing when he left you behind," said Cameron.

"He didn't leave me! He merely accepted a more
challenging position at IBM in another state. That's all.
Don't get it twisted," argued Raven.

"Oh, is that what he told you?" teased Cameron.

"Anyway, don't come over here trying to pour salt
on your boy. He's not here to defend himself remember,"
said Raven.

"I'm not. I'm just saying, what kind of man would
leave his woman behind like that," questioned Cameron.

"No, the question is what kind of man would fool
around with his best friends' woman? That is the real
question," asked Raven.

"Okay, don't start. You didn't have to go there. I feel bad enough about the situation as it is. I should have never introduced you to him," said Cameron remorsefully.

"Why are you here Cameron? It's 11 o'clock at night and you really should be at home."

Cameron rarely stopped by just to talk. There was always a hidden agenda. Whatever Cameron wanted Cameron normally got. He was an investment broker who was accustomed to driving results in both his professional and personal life. His often impudent and overly aggressive demeanor was just a facade though. It was the shield he needed to be successful in his line of work. Once you got past the defensive exterior, he was gentle and profoundly passionate in his own way.

He had proven over the years to be very thoughtful by never forgetting to call or send a gift on her birthday. He made sure he always wished Raven a Happy Valentine's

Day, Thanksgiving, and a Merry Christmas. He always knew the right things to say and do at the right time. About four years ago, a popular music entertainer was scheduled to come to town and Raven desperately wanted to go. Cameron decided to surprise her and bought front row tickets for them to attend on Valentine's Day. The night would have been perfect had he not decided to bring his wife along. The three of them sat awkwardly together at the round table drinking, laughing and trying to enjoy the evening.

"I told you already. I wanted to see you. Now turn around and let me get a good look at you girl."

"Stop it…No, that's not it. Jared must have mentioned that I am going to see him next Monday."

"Well, yeah, he did mention something like that the other day. But that's not why I'm here. Let me show you why I'm here."

Raven's heart began to race as he reached out his arm to draw her nearer. His touch was warm and endearing. She could not bring herself to turn away. His embrace grew stronger as he escorted her into the living room. She wanted him to brace her against the foyer wall and take her right there – right now. As his hands began gently fondling her breasts, she glided her hand down the outer seam of his pants and started stroking him. Up and down, up and down. Each stroke gradually becoming more forceful and passionate than the one before. Her breathing grew heavier and deeper as lust thickened the air. Carefully she worked her hand around the curvature of his brawny physique towards his inner thigh to welcome her longtime friend with a smile.

"Oh, now I see why you're here. Someone is happy to see me...Hello, my friend."

She let out a childish giggle, followed by a consenting moan. Raven knew then that she would soon regret what she had allowed herself to succumb to time after time. Although she dreaded the loneliness that would greet her after he hugged and kissed her goodbye, all that mattered to her now was this very moment that they shared. Over the years, they had created a sacred union that was filled with adoration and mutual understanding. He did more for her than just fill the void of Jared's absence.

Cameron massaged away Raven's doubts and worries leaving her feeling desired and cherished. And Raven reciprocated his affection by stroking his ego and being both a friend and lover to him. He could not deny his strong feelings for Raven no matter how hard he tried. They were soul mates and complemented each other in ways no one else could understand. It was a different type of union, but it was theirs, nonetheless. A soul tie that could never be broken.

As her nipples began shyly peeping through her long black silk nightgown, they pierced against Cameron's chest. The summer heat seeped through the screen door and wrapped itself around her legs. It caused her gown to cling tighter to her body although soon it would find itself tossed aside on the floor. While grasping her silky thighs, Cameron slowly took her naked body and braced her upon his throne. Lusting for her was something that he enjoyed every minute of. His controlling nature dominated the mood as she humbly followed his lead. Sounds of passion filled the room as he repeatedly thrashed himself inside of her taboo tunnel. It was as if he had waited years for this moment to arrive and now that it was here, he was unstoppable.

Desire grew stronger with every stroke. As he became more engrossed in the moment, he gently laid her upon her back and began exploring her inner beauty. Dimly lit candles illuminated the hallway and revealed shadows of naked images dancing along the corridor. While she lay on the marble tile flooring that lined the foyer, the taste of her love dripped from his lips and left him hungrier than

before. Only the rise and fall of her hips and the flow of her

juices could help quench his hunger for passion. She could

still feel the sultry breeze through the screen door as it

grazed across her firm nipples and fondled her skin. The

heat of the moment silenced the sound of chanting crickets

in the distance and caused her to focus on the chocolate

brute that lay feasting between her moistened thighs.

"Cameron, I - - I..."

"Sshhh...don't say a word." He raised his fingers to

her warm, soft lips and she began tasting the love of her

own. Ecstasy took control of her speech and left her knees

shaking uncontrollably. Tears began running down her

cheeks as guilt set it. Thoughts of Jared raced through her

mind while Cameron flowed through her body. How could

she face Jared after sharing such a sinful moment with his

best friend – yet again? But she could not help herself. She

was victimized by his charm and sexual advances every

time she came in contact with him. Her flesh was weak for him.

Maybe if she told Jared he would somehow understand the reason behind her infidelity, she thought. Whom was she kidding? She did not even understand it herself, so how was she going to convince Jared that this love affair was just something that she needed and could not resist. That somehow her relationship with Cameron had grown to a deeper level over the years than she ever imagined or could begin to explain. He had become a part of her, and she would not be complete without him in her life. Jared would not and could not understand the bond that had transformed over all of these years. Nor was it fair to expect him to.

"Please baby. Stop…we can't do this." It pained her to utter those words, but it would hurt even more if she lost Jared because she lacked self-control. She did not want to tarnish the moment, but this thing she had with Cameron had lingered on for years and deep down she wanted it to either stop or move forward in another direction. She knew that he would never leave his wife, even if he had hinted around filing for a divorce on several occasions. At this point in her life, Raven was not so sure she would even want him if he went through with it.

Sometimes she thought that maybe she had seen too much, felt too much, and knew too much about him to make things work. Although she secretly enjoyed the cat-mouse chase and the discreet rendezvous, she knew that this could not go on forever. It would all have to come to an end one day if she was ever planning on a long-term commitment with Jared. But how would this affair with Cameron end? That was the question she had toiled with repeatedly but could never find the answer. She was not even sure she wanted to know the answer.

"What do you mean stop?" Cameron questioned.

Cameron knew just what she wanted. She always enjoyed the pleasure he brought her. He was intuitive to her needs and sensitive areas. He loved to hear her erotic screams and moans of passion echo throughout the room. It fed his ego and drove him to give her more of himself.

"I mean stop it!" Raven demanded as she pulled herself from under his muscular hold.

"We can't go on giving in to temptation every time our eyes meet. It's not right. It's just not right," she pleaded. "Jared would kill us both if he ever found out!"

"Well, babe, that's why some things you just have to take to your grave. I mean, it is what it is, right? I just can't stop loving you, babe. Nor do I want to. You feel so good and I – "

"—and you what, Cameron? And you can't get this kind of loving at home? You always seem to forget about your wife! You know—Monica! What do you tell her as you stroll your ass in at four o'clock in the morning

anyway? Got lost?!"

"Look! Monica has nothing to do with this. This is

all about me, you and this moment right here. I make you

happy, don't I? Don't I give you what you need and when

you need it?"

"Yes, you make me very happy. But there's—"

"Well then, let's just enjoy this night together. Then

when you get back from New Jersey if you want to call

things off, I'll understand."

Raven knew better. As controlling as Cameron was,

there was no way he was letting her out of this relationship

that easy. Whenever things finally came to an end it would

have to be on his terms and his terms only.

As the night dwindled away, the two of them shared

a few more moments of close touching and embracing.

Conversations of their love for each other and sexual

fantasies entertained them throughout the remainder of the night.

Brrinnnggg…Brrrrinnnggg. "Is that the phone," Raven spoke out into the darkness as she raised up from a deep sleep. She glanced over at the antique clock she received as a gift for her twenty-fifth birthday from Cameron. It read 4:18 a.m. "Who would be calling me at this hour," she mumbled.

"It's probably Jared," answered Cameron. "Don't tell him I'm here 'cause he might start trippin'," he mumbled sarcastically in his morning baritone voice.

"Or maybe Monica has finally figured out where you spend all of your time."

How she wished for a voice other than Jared's at the other end of the receiver. Maybe it would be the wrong number; someone looking for the Best 1 Cab Company across town. Or perhaps it would be for the couple that occupied her number six months ago who apparently never paid their bills on time. Or maybe Brandi was calling to tell her about her blind date with the lawyer-dude last night. Whoever it was she hoped it was not Jared. It would be difficult to hold an honest conversation with Cameron's hand resting between her thighs.

"Hello…" she uttered in a soft and somewhat sensual voice.

"Hey baby… Did I wake you," questioned Jared?

"Hi sweetie. Yeah, I was sleeping…uh…what's going on," she said as whispers of guilt soared through her head.

"I know it's early, but I was just laying here thinking about you and how much I can't wait to see you tomorrow."

"Ooh, isn't that sweet. I know. I can't wait to see you either. It's been a while," she said as she lay still next to Cameron praying that he did not make a sound. This was not the first time that she had been in an awkward situation like this. Jared had called many times before while his best friend was over entertaining without his knowledge. This particular morning was no different.

"Yeah, I miss you so much. I'll be there waiting for you when your flight arrives."

"You better…you better not keep me waiting long either." Cameron's hand began exploring the region around her upper inner thigh. She wiggled to get him to move his hand, but he was persistent and continued caressing her forbidden zones.

"Oh, I won't baby. You don't have to worry about that. I've got somewhere special I want to take you as soon as you land."

It was getting harder to resist the throbbing temptation that she felt between her thighs. His tongue was now circling around her belly button as she lay nakedly

exposed. She needed to end this call soon; otherwise she

may lose her composure.

"Well, I'm sure it will be some place nice. I look

forward to whatever it is. Well, I better go. I want to get a

couple more hours sleep before I get up and go shopping.

I've got a few more things to pick up before I fly out

tomorrow."

They ended the call with their routine I-love-you's

and good-bye's and she began one last round with Cameron

before he headed home.

As dawn began fighting with the meekness of night

for control, Raven realized that she was just hours away

from seeing Jared. Brandi should arrive any moment to

pick her up and take her to the airport. The time had flown

by so fast that it was hard to believe the day of her trip had

finally arrived. It had been six months since she last saw

him. He flew to Chicago for a business convention at McCormick Place. Although he was only visiting for a few days, they managed to take in some sights, attend a play, go out to dinner a few times, and make love for hours on end. Travel sex, as Raven called it, was the best.

"She's here!" Raven sighed as Brandi pulled up alongside the curb. She quickly grabbed her pieces of Louis Vuitton luggage and made her way to the car.

"Hey girl! Are you all ready to see your man?"

"Yeah, looking forward to it. You know it's been awhile," Raven said as she stuffed her luggage into the small sized trunk. Raven adored Brandi's gold BMW whose plates read: AU DIGGR, but the trunk was never big enough to hold their bags. Whenever they went on one of their shopping excursions, they would have to lay the back seats down so they could fit all of their purchases in the back.

"Yeah, I know. But what I really want to know is what Cameron had to say about you flying out this morning. I know he either stopped by or called you last night. He was probably blowing up your phone! That's why you're looking a hot mess this morning," joked Brandi.

"What? What's wrong with how I look? You don't like this outfit? This is one of Jared's favorite outfits. He loves the way these pants hug my hips."

"Yeah, I know, but Cameron bought it for you! So, I guess they both love it! Boy, I tell you. If I could be half the player you are, I would be doing good."

"Just get me to the airport please. You can live vicariously through my life some other time," Raven said in laughter.

"We are now boarding flight number 657 leaving from Chicago to Newark non-stop," announced the flight attendant. That's me, she thought. The moment had finally arrived, and she was just moments away from seeing Jared. She gathered her carry-on bag and started heading towards the ticket counter. Bbbbzzzzz…Bbbbzzzzzzzz. She reached down to see who was sending her a text message on her cellular phone.

"Hey sexy! N bed n my bday suit. Wish u were here. Miss u already! Call me when u get back".

It was Cameron.

"So, where are you taking me, Jared?" As hard as she tried to make small talk the suspense was killing her.

"Calm down and be patient. I just have something I want to show you. We'll be there shortly."

"Well, maybe I could calm down if my eyes weren't blindfolded. You know I don't like surprises, Jared."

The road they were traveling felt much different than before. Last time she came to visit she remembered turning off the express way and heading down 42nd Street

about six blocks before turning right near Pauly's Pizzeria.
From there they drove about four more blocks to the row of
brownstones near an elementary school, which was around
the corner. At this hour of the morning she would have
expected the streets to have been littered with crowded
buses and rambunctious children eager to make their way
to school. But instead, the streets were quiet, almost too
quiet. Where were the buses? Why weren't there any
children laughing and chanting elementary school rhymes?

Raven could recall the joys of playing double-dutch
on the corner with her classmates in the morning. One
package of heavy-duty clothesline was all three kids needed
to have some early morning fun while waiting for the bus
to arrive. 'Miss Mary Mack, Mack, Mack…all dressed in
black, black, black…with silver buttons…buttons…buttons
all down her back, back, back…' was chanted over and
over as each girl took her turn jumping and twirling
through the skips and beats of the clothesline cord.

Tick…tick…tick went the sound of the cord hitting the pavement, all while the youthful wrists continued turning in perfect harmony. Looking back, it appeared to be an innate skill that some girls possessed because there really was no formal training provided to aspiring youths on how to double-dutch. Nor was there a right or a wrong way to jump. In this sporting event, creativity was crucial. Each girl touted her ability to move, jump, hop, and twirl like no other on the block. Creating moves as she went along and passing them off as if she had practiced them for months. Ahhh, those were the days, Raven thought, when life was simple.

Now her life was complicated. More complicated than she ever imagined it would be. She was in love, or so she thought, with two men. Two men that happened to be best friends. Where had the youthful and innocently simplistic life gone?

"Okay, we're here. But wait a minute. Don't take off the blind fold just yet. I am going to get the door for you."

"Oh my! You are really pouring on the charm this morning. What did I do to deserve this royal treatment?"

She slowly stepped out of the car and began following Jared's lead towards the front door. She went up a few steps but noticed the railing was no longer within her reach. Instead her hand met the likes of a thorny rose bush. This sure did not feel like the townhouse she visited just last December.

As she began to step across the threshold Jared swept her off her feet and carried her into the great room. He carefully lowered her to her feet and untied the blindfold that had remained intact for the last hour.

"Welcome home, babe," he whispered softly in her ear.

Tears began to form in Raven's eyes as she spun around the room taking in all its splendor. She could hardly believe that Jared bought his house just last week in hopes that she would move in with him. She ran frantically from room to room checking out the picturesque views and ample closet space. It was a contemporary four-bedroom house with arched entryways, vaulted ceilings, a loft, and a three-car garage. Jared had a motorcycle and a Tesla so the extra space would be reserved for Raven's Lexus. Jared was adamant about having an entire parking space for his motorcycle, whereas some men would be content with occupying a portion of a parking space, but not Jared. His bike was his prize possession and it warranted him spending extra money for a house with a three-car garage so that his other baby would be comfortable year-round.

"I love it! I love it!" she screamed from the master bedroom which had a two-sided fireplace that could be enjoyed from either the master bath or master bedroom suite. The master bath had limestone tile throughout, a deep whirlpool bathtub and a separate shower with six movable heads positioned on multiple walls that would surely make for some interesting fore or after play. She could just picture herself lying on his king-sized bed, champagne flutes in hand, listening to the crackling sound of the fireplace and enjoying each other's company. It was gorgeous, simply gorgeous.

"I was hoping that we could go shopping for some furniture later this afternoon," Jared shouted back. "Raven…Raven…do you hear me up there? You know we're not too far from downtown or the fashion district. I know how much you like to shop. And there is plenty of closet space up there for all your shoes. And if the closets overflow, don't worry there is even more space in the attic. Hey—What are you doing up there?"

As Jared slowly turned around to face the spiral staircase, he caught a glimpse of a silhouette out the corner of his eye. Raven was standing at the top of the stairs bearing only her belly button piercing and matching toe ring. Her onyx-colored hair was parted down the middle and flowing down her back.

"Does this mean you'll move in?" Jared said with a smile that showed all thirty-two of his pearly whites.

"I would like to test the place out first to make sure it suites my needs. If you know what I mean," Raven said with a sinfully tempting smile.

Jared raced over to meet his caramel-colored goddess who stood poised and ready to inaugurate each area of the house on command. He dashed up the stairs and lunged hungrily towards her like a lion going after its innocuous prey. He took Raven from behind forcing her to hold firmly to the wooden banister. She arched her back, leaned slightly forward and let her head dangle aimlessly towards the first floor where the sun was awakening from its night long rest. It darted across the hard wood floors and

made its way to the kitchen illuminating everything in its

path, taking no prisoners. As Raven stood there

outstretched and sprawled, Jared began kissing the small of

her back; gradually going lower with each kiss.

With his hands clenched on the sides of her hips,

Raven began swaying from side to side creating a motion

that Jared soon reciprocated. Their harmonious dance took

them to the floor of the loft then to the bedroom near the

fireplace and on to the kitchen where they finally ended

their housewarming rendezvous on the cool ceramic tile.

The night was young, and the wind was a brute, but

Jared wanted to take Raven out on the town to celebrate her

arrival and the purchase of the home. He was excited to

finally have Raven near him. It had been so long since he

last saw her. At times he felt as if the two of them were

drifting apart and this bothered him more than he led on.

Now acclimated in his new position at IBM he was ready to

settle down and raise a family, but he was not so sure

Raven felt the same. The sex was good but at this point in

his life he wanted so much more. He wanted a companion;

someone who would be at his side every waking morning.

He wanted a wife. He needed to talk to her and hear what

she wanted.

Raven was a vegetarian so Jared always found it

difficult to find restaurants whose menu would fancy them

both. After much debate, they agreed upon a quaint Thai

restaurant over on 143rd Street. They ordered their entrees,

sipped champagne and chatted about recent movies each

had recently seen. They spoke briefly of their jobs and

different projects they were working on but made a point

not to dwell on the topic for too long. Discussing work was

something that they both frowned on. It drained the

conversation and usually caused the other to get worked up

over their lack of pay, recognition, long hours, or obtuse

co-workers who always managed to get the promotions and flexible schedules they felt they deserved.

The evening was going well but something was missing. Raven was having the time of her life, yet something did not feel right. Was it something in the way Jared mischievously glanced over at his watch from time to time during their conversation as if he had some other place to be? Or maybe it was something in the way Jared stared blankly across the room while Raven spoke of playful banter between her and her friends. Something had him preoccupied and it was obviously not Raven's conversation.

"Are you okay? You don't seem yourself tonight?" questioned Raven.

"No, I'm fine. I've just got a lot of things on my mind right now. I'm sorry. What were you saying?"

"I was asking you if you were ready to go. I think the movie starts soon and – "

Jared's phone rings and he stares down to see who is calling but does not answer it.

"Who's that?" Raven asks.

"Oh, it's nobody," he says as he turns his ringer off. "I'm ready to go. Let's get out of here."

The ride to the theatre was uncomfortably quiet. The silence in the air was filled with tension and uncertainty. Raven desperately wanted to find out who had called him earlier during dinner, but she did not want to pry or appear rattled by the event. Besides, she was not sure she could handle the truth if he told her. If it was another woman what could she say or do anyway? She was not in a position to comment on his affairs when she was guilty of the same sinful pleasures.

Looking back, she could remember a time when Jared was in town visiting and Cameron called wanting to come over. He knew that Jared was in town but loved seeing how far he could go without getting caught. It was around one o'clock in the morning when the phone rang. She was not sure who it was but hoped that it was not Cameron. She fumbled for the phone in the dark and tried to quickly answer it before Jared awoke. After a couple of hello's and who's there she hung up leaving Jared to believe it was the wrong number.

Although Jared did not mention the incident at breakfast the next morning, he appeared a bit reserved. When asked what he had planned for the day he only responded with a shrug of the shoulders and kept his head down as he read the morning headlines. There was no kiss goodbye at the door. No smiles and no exchange of words. Only a long stare that uttered more than his lips could ever say. Later that afternoon Raven awaited a call from Jared;

but nothing. She figured maybe he was in meetings most of the day and did not have a moment to check in on her. Surely, he would call her tonight. Nothing. Actually, Raven did not hear from Jared for the next four days. Not a word. No phone call, no emails, and no text messages. Each time she tried to reach him; her call was directed straight to his voicemail box.

They had finally arrived at the theater. The line outside was long so Jared decided to drop Raven off at the door and find a park. He found a parking space far from the theater and other cars. He was always cautious about where he parked his car and did not mind walking long distances as long as his car would not get scratched by runaway shopping carts or car doors.

While Jared was parking the car, Raven decided to send Cameron a quick text message letting him know she was thinking about him.

"Thinkn bout u… C u soon!"

She hesitated for a moment. Should she really be sending such a message while spending time with Jared? In her own spiteful way, she thought yes. Who knows who he was avoiding earlier when he did not answer his phone, she thought? For all she knew he was keeping his options open and it was another woman on the other line that he was brushing off for the moment. Her thumb hung over the send button on her cell phone for a brief moment. She quickly sent the message as she saw Jared out the corner of her eye running towards the theater to get in line next to her.

Cameron did not text back. He must be with his wife, she thought.

Even though it made her feel like a hypocrite, she could not resist the urge to ask Jared about the call he received earlier. She decided to wait until the car ride home before she brought it up. For now, she would just sit back and enjoy the show.

On the way back home from movies Raven could not resist the temptation to inquire about the deflected call Jared received earlier. "So, who called you when we were at the restaurant?" questioned Raven hoping he would be truthful but at the same time not sure how she would handle his response.

"What are you talking about?"

"You know…right before we left the restaurant, I noticed someone called you but you did not answer it."

Jared seemed annoyed by her line of questioning. They were having an enjoyable evening of dinner and a movie and he was not in the mood for an argument or her insecurities.

"Do you really think I would have brought you out here, bought us a house only to cheat on you, Raven? Are you serious?"

"Who said anything about cheating? Are you cheating on me," her voice becoming sterner by the moment?

"Of course I'm not!" Jared yelled. "Why in the world would I do that? You're tripping."

"It's just that…well…ummm…I just don't understand why you didn't answer it. What am I supposed to think?" She was trying not to sound as accusatory as she knew she probably was coming across.

"You're supposed to trust me like I trust you. Are you cheating on me back home with some dude? How do I really know what you're doing or who you have over there when I call you?"

What was he implying, she thought to herself? Did Jared suspect that Cameron was over to her house the times he would call late at night? How could he have possibly known? They always made a point to make sure Cameron barely took a breath let alone utter a word. Must be a coincidence or her guilt surfacing at the most inopportune time. She had to pull herself together and turn this conversation around. After all, she really was in no position to question anything he did. He bought her a house. True. He constantly told and showed her he loved her. True. But why did she not trust him? She needed more evidence, she thought. A misplaced earring, a bottle of floral-scented body wash or lotion left in the bathroom by mistake, or anything that would prove her suspicions to be true.

"You're right. I'm tripping. Maybe I am just tired from the travel out here. I apologize."

"Hmmmhh…yea," said Jared with a bit of disgust in his voice.

"Do you forgive me?" said Raven in a sultry, and seductive voice. "Please forgive me." Jared remained silent, keeping his eyes on the road. He refused to entertain her insecurities and line of questioning. He just wanted to get home and put this moment behind them both.

"Why don't you pull over up there," said Raven as she pointed to a somewhat empty lot off to the right-hand side of the road.

"And why would I do that? I just want to get home. I think it's been a long day for both of us."

"Just do it, please. Pretty please," Raven pleaded. Grudgingly Jared pulls over and turns off the car.

"What now? Are you finally happy?"

The streetlight near them was flickering on and off barely illuminating the few empty cars in the lot. The dark tint made it hard to see in or out of the car windows.

Raven reached over and turned on the radio. She scrolled to her favorite playlist and began streaming tunes by The Weeknd.

"I don't want to hear any music. I just want to go home."

"Aww, c'mon Jared. Like you said, it's been a long day. Let's just sit here for a minute, okay?"

Jared looked into her eyes and immediately folded. There was something magical and mysterious about Raven's eyes that he could not explain. They were intriguing, enticing, and brought an unshakable fear to him all at the same time. 'Eyes are the window to one's soul,' they say, but he struggled to make sense of what he saw when he gazed into her eyes. At times they felt cold and restrictive with a neon light flashing DO NOT ENTER, while other times they were warm and inviting evoking him to want to dive in and swim with her in deep waters. Not knowing where the depth of those waters would take him is what he worried about most.

To completely trust Raven meant allowing himself to be vulnerable and willing to accept the unknown and uncontrollable emotions. While in the back of his mind he could not help thinking about her close friendship with Cameron. Although he never mentioned or questioned their relationship, he always had his doubts. Sure, Cameron was his boy and they'd known each other most of their lives but he was a man and men, like women, are not always loyal. The curious part of him wanted to know more but the boyish part of him didn't think he could handle knowing whatever their truths revealed. There was a bit of solace in the not knowing that he was not ready to relinquish. Sometimes he would catch Raven staring off into the distance, her mind appearing to be many miles away. He often wondered what was flowing through her mind, if she was reminiscing about a memory she shared with someone else from her past or present. He did not want to control her thoughts, but only wanted to understand them.

"So, what do you want to talk about, Raven? What's on your mind?"

"I just want to be present in this moment with you. Right here, right now," she said while gently rubbing his leg. "It really is good to see you. I know things have been crazy between us with the distance, our careers and everything but I am committed to us. I want this relationship to continue to grow. We've got a good thing, babe. So, let's just enjoy our time together and not let foolish thoughts get in the way. What do you say?"

Jared faked a sincere smile and agreed. The rest of the ride home was peaceful. Only the mellow sounds of The Weekend filled the silence between them. Jared kept his eyes on the road while Raven stared off into the distance towards the city lights.

Later that night, Raven received a text message. Jared was in the bathroom shaving but could hear her phone chime. It was Cameron. He knew Raven was visiting Jared but missed her; her scent, her smile, her lips - both sets of them, and the convenience of stopping by her house unannounced.

"Hey you…", said Cameron

Raven stared at her phone for a few seconds. Hesitant to respond she quickly turned her volume off and hid any incoming alerts from Cameron's number. One thing was for sure, she was not going to get caught up on this trip because of Cameron. She couldn't risk receiving any late-night phone calls or text messages from him. It would be too hard to explain to Jared why Cameron was messaging her at 2:00 am. And what if he asked to see the text message or demanded she answer or call him back. It would be tough to play out the 'wrong phone number' act this time.

There was no good ending to either of the scenarios that played out in her head. Cameron had a wife, a safe haven. If things did not work out between him and Raven then he could always find comfort in the arms of Monica, leaving Raven by herself. She glanced at her phone again but made no sudden moves to respond. She inhaled deeply, taking in all the thoughts of her lustful night with Cameron before she boarded the plane. Then she exhaled, trying to make sense of all the frustrations of the love-triangle life she helped create and was remorsefully a part of.

"Call Monica when you can", texted Cameron, "she wants to invite you somewhere."

Monica wants to invite me somewhere, Raven thought. Oh boy, here we go. Cameron was always trying to control Raven's life, her circle of friends, her relationship with Jared, how she spent her down time— anything within his reach. A few weeks ago, he suggested that she and Monica plan a girl's trip to Miami. Monica was from Ohio and did not have many friends in the area, or period for that matter. She was an introvert who preferred reading more than interacting with people. She was very intelligent but socially awkward. Cameron thought it would be good for Raven to hang out with her from time to time. He thought she could help Monica loosen up a bit, laugh and enjoy more of what life had to offer.

How could she spend a weekend with her lover's wife with a clear conscience? Not possible, she thought, but Cameron had a persuasive way of convincing even the most stubborn person to go along with his ideas. They'd spent Valentine's Day together at the comedy show years ago but Raven was not interested in getting that close with the enemy again. She liked the distance shared between her and Monica. It kept her from dwelling on reality. With Monica out of sight and mind, the infidelity did not sound alarms for concern. It was just the way it was and there was no need to stop doing what made them both feel amazing in the moment.

"Who was that?" questioned Jared.

"Who was what?" responded Raven.

"I heard your phone go off. Is that Brandi bugging you again? Why can't she just let you enjoy your time with me. I'm sure you'll give her the blow-by-blow details once you get back."

"Ha! No, it wasn't Brandi. It was Cameron. He said that Monica is trying to reach me. I'll call her later."

"Monica? What do you think she wants?"

"Ummm...I don't know. Cameron mentioned something the other week about it being a good idea for me and her to take a girl's trip. But I don't know. She's kind of boring, you know?"

"You're so judgmental, Raven. Everybody can't be as entertaining as you. I think it's a good idea. You could use a vacation," said Jared, "and she's not that bad."

"Well, I thought I was on a vacation now. With all the pampering you've been doing it feels like a baecation or something," laughed Raven.

"No, sweetie. You are home - or at least I want this to be your home. I want you to experience me each and every day. Do you remember when we first met, and I told you that you were my last first kiss?"

"Yes, I remember. You were running a lot of game on me back then," laughed Raven, "I was young and naive."

"Well, it wasn't game, babe. I meant it."

"You always know just the right thing to say to get me glowing," said Raven. Jared was a soul snatcher. He could snatch the soul right out of Raven with just a few simple and sincere words. He'd been doing it for years and she wondered if, over time, she'd even have a soul left to snatch.

"Okay, you're right. It could be fun. Maybe Brandi might want to join us, too. I will give her a call tomorrow morning before we head to the beach."

Jared walked over to the side of the bed where Raven was sitting. With only a towel wrapped around his waist and beads of water glistening on his dominant chest, he gently kissed her on the forehead. Rubbing his hand alongside her cheek, he leaned closer and whispered into her ear, "My sun rises and sets with you. You're my anything and everything. Remember that."

How could she forget. While he was not perfect and was prone to occasional mood swings, Jared was the one who completed her life. She did not want to imagine a life without him, or so she said to herself because if she really feared losing Jared then why did she always allow herself to be a jester in Cameron's side show. Over the years, she convinced herself that she was truly in love with two men but as time went on, she questioned if that was even possible. It did not seem feasible to equally love two men at the same time. The way she saw it, someone had to be loved a little less than the other and whomever she loved least is the one that she needed to stop seeing. Constantly torn between the scales of love and logic, she trudges through the days unable to reckon a solution. Everything will work itself out, she tells herself. It always does.

"Hi, Monica. It's Raven. Cameron asked me to give you a call. How are you?

"Hi Raven! Thanks for calling. I am doing well. How is your trip going so far? I heard you were visiting Jared this weekend in Jersey."

A little bit of Raven cringed inside when questioned by Monica. She thought it humorous how Cameron always picked and choose what information to share with Monica about his life. Why did he need to tell her that Raven was visiting Jared? Was it so she would think that there was nothing going on between him and Raven? Instead, why didn't he share how he likes for Raven to show up at the door naked, covered only in glittered oil when he arrives late at night. Or how he likes to wrap his tie around her neck so she can crawl slowly on her hands and knees as he pulls her down the foyer hallway from the front door towards the bedroom.

Growing more and more excited as she moans with every step. Or how he devours Raven while bending her over on the chaise lounge, legs spread wide apart, tasting her incessantly. No, he would never reveal his sexual encounters with Monica. He would only keep harmlessly deflecting the truths about his relationship with Raven in hopes of never getting caught.

"I am having a great time! I fly back tomorrow. Thanks for asking," said Raven trying to hide the uncomfortableness in her voice.

"That's great to hear, Raven. I wanted to see if you were still interested in taking a trip to Miami next month."

"Yea, sure. That sounds like fun. Just let me know the dates you were thinking, and I'll be sure to take off from work. Hey, do you mind if Brandi joins us?" The thought of Raven spending time on the beach with her lover's wife was the most disturbing thought any woman could have. To lie on a beach towel in a bikini next to Monica while fantasizing about her husband partaking in the fruit between her thighs was self-torture. At least with Brandi there she could help keep her sinful thoughts at bay and actually enjoy the time away.

"I would love it if she could join us! She is a lot of fun. Okay, I will text you the dates tomorrow. I am so excited!"

Excitement was not the emotion Raven was feeling as she disconnected the call. Bewilderment maybe, but definitely not excited to have a mistress and wife weekend getaway. The thought seemed to make for a suspenseful Lifetime movie where in the end the mistress is found dead, washed up on shore with a lot of speculation around 'who dun it' and why. Not exactly the fairytale ending she hoped for and definitely an ending she hoped to avoid.

The next couple of weeks went by fast. The girls were planning to leave the following weekend for Miami, which was only six days away. Monica suggested they all get together to go swimsuit shopping at the mall. Grudgingly, Raven accepted the invite and forced Brandi to accompany them.

"How do you think this looks on me, Raven," questioned Monica.

"I think red is more your color. Why don't you try this one, Monica?"

"Oh wow, look at you Brandi! The women won't be able to keep their men off you in that bikini," proclaimed Monica.

"You think so? You think this looks okay? You know I'm not going to be out there trying to steal anyone's husband or anything but, well...you know," teased Brandi.

Brandi turned and looked at Raven with a smirk. Raven kindly returned the facial gesture. At times, Brandi could be so petty and always got a kick out of instigating situations. She was Raven's best friend, tried and true, but sometimes she wished she could put a muzzle on her mouth to keep her from saying everything that came to her mind.

"Yea, looks like there will be some husband-snatching on the beach for sure with that one," commented Raven. Why not join in the playful banter, she thought. She knew she did not need a micro-bikini or a beach scene in Miami to snag Cameron. Just a little oil, crotchless panties and perfume and he came running like a dog in heat every time.

"Oh, would you look at this? Cameron is so frisky at times. He wants me to send him pics of my top three swimsuits," said Monica.

Frisky, huh, Raven thought. No, Monica he just wants to make sure you don't choose anything too revealing because he does not want men gawking at you the way he gawks at me. Raven, on the other hand, is too smart for that. She already picked out the swimsuit shot to send him which was not the swimsuit she planned on taking with her to Miami. Sometimes you have to outsmart the fox at their own game.

"Awww, how sweet. He's getting all excited about seeing you in your beach best," said Brandi.

"Yea, I'm going to send him a couple of pics and then I should probably head home. He says he has something special planned for us tonight."

This was another game that Cameron loved to play called Raven Revenge where he attempted to upset Raven for hurting him. In this instance, he was upset that she went to visit Jared and did not keep in contact with him while she was gone. It was a power thing with him. He felt that no matter what they should always be able to stay connected. His ego was scarred, and he wanted her to feel what he felt. He didn't care if his wife was right there or if Jared was nearby. He wanted Raven whenever he wanted her with no excuses or obstacles.

On the ride home from the mall Raven's phone rang. It was Cameron.

"Think I should answer it?"

"Naw, let that dude go to voicemail, girl," joked Brandi.

After about one minute the rings stopped. A few minutes later her phone rang again. It was Cameron. He was persistent and touted a 'I will not be denied' persona.

"I think I better answer it. Otherwise this will go on all night and he'll end up at my doorstep."

"Hello."

"What's wrong with your phone," questioned Cameron.

"Nothing. What are you taking about?"

"Well, something must be wrong with it because my calls are not getting through. And I KNOW you are not sitting there watching my calls go to voicemail," said Cameron in a stern voice.

"Look, I've been busy since I got back. Had to get settled from my vacation with Jared and these last few days I've been preparing for the trip with Monica. So, what is your problem?"

"Oh yea, your trip with my boy. You must have had a really, really good time because I couldn't seem to get a hold of either one of you."

"What are you talking about?"

"I called him while you were out there, and he kept sending my calls to voicemail. That's some punk ass shit but whatever. I ain't gone sweat that. I was just trying to holla at my boy, but I guess you had him all tied up and shit."

So, Cameron was the one who kept calling Jared while she was visiting. All this time she thought it was some other woman. She should have known that Cameron would try to infiltrate their time together. Nothing was beneath him when it came to Raven. He wanted what he wanted, when he wanted it. With his calls and texts silenced on Raven's phone, she was not aware of his messages until she checked them at the airport on her way back to Chicago.

She had well over twenty-five text messages over the course of two days. He went on and on about how he missed her and wanted to see her as soon as she returned. Even offering to pick her up from the airport in hopes that they could stop to make love in the car along the highway. While tempting, Raven decided not to accept his offer and avoid any contact with him. She felt it would only make her vacation with Monica even more awkward. The way she rationalized it in her mind, she wasn't really cheating with Cameron if she hadn't slept with him a couple of weeks before her vacation with Monica. At that point it was past tense and not a current affair. It was the only logical way for her to make it through the next few days in Miami, so

she convinced herself and went on with the illusion of
fidelity.

"I don't know why he didn't answer your calls. But
you knew I was out there visiting so why were you calling
anyway?"

"You know I've gotta see what you're up to, Raven.
I can't have you out there talking about marriage and all
that mess. My heart couldn't take it. You know that. I love
you, girl," pleaded Cameron.

"Cameron, you are so full of it. Why would you
even care if I married Jared or anyone else for that matter.
You have a wife! I don't know why you keep forgetting
that."

"Awww, that ain't nothing. You know we are on
the verge of not being together. So, I don't even know why
you brought that up. You are the one for me, Raven, and

you know that. Can't nobody break this bond we've got. Nobody."

That was the kind of talk that lured and disgusted Raven at the same time. She agreed that the bond between them was strong and at times seemed unbreakable, but it was built on lies and deceit. She was smart enough to know that you cannot have a healthy relationship if the foundation was built on quicksand. The day would never come where they could announce to the world that they were a couple and force everyone to accept their union and erase any doubt about its formation. Curious minds would wander and think back to every moment they were in each other's presence and how they must have been dating while he was married and while she led Jared on thinking they might marry one day.

Those thoughts would continually torture Monica and Jared because that type of betrayal is hard to forget; almost impossible. They did not deserve that kind of emotional abuse nor did Raven and Cameron wish to inflict any pain upon them. But how and when would this cat and mouse chase end, she would often ponder. As much as she wanted it to be over, the thrill of it made her want it to go on. It pleased her in ways that were indescribable and incomprehensible to anyone outside their union. What they shared could only be put into emotions and not words. Physical touch and not complete sentences. It was a twisted love language interpreted only by a gifted few; none of which were Jared or Monica.

"Okay, Cameron, whatever you say. I'm almost home. I will talk to you later."

"No, you'll see me later. I'm coming through."

Only six days until her girl's trip. She wanted desperately to hold off seeing him until she returned but he was persistent as always.

"I am not sure that's a good idea. I am tired and have an early start tomorrow."

"You'll be fine. I'll see you in a bit. Wear something sexy or nothing at all," he commanded. It was like the old E.F. Hutton commercials. When Cameron spoke, Raven and everyone else listened.

Cameron never took no for an answer. It was pointless to think she could even tell him no. He knew what buttons to push and how to pry his way past any objection she could fathom. If he wanted sexy, then she was going to give him sexy tonight.

The doorbell rings followed by an erratic knock at the door.

Raven gracefully makes her way to the door dressed in a red lingerie ensemble. As she opens the door, Cameron barges in questioning what took her so long.

"Look, I don't want any problems with you tonight, okay. Don't come in here tripping. You can go right back home if that's what you came to do," said Raven.

"I'm sorry, babe. It's just that I miss you and I haven't had my medicine. You know how crazy I get when I haven't had my medicine."

Drawing her closer to his chest, he inhaled the exotic scent lingering on her neck. Slowly his nose followed the scent down to her cleavage. "Mmmmhhhh, that's what I am talking about, girl. My medicine. You know I need a dose of you. I don't know why you be playing with me...staying gone all long and avoiding my calls and messages. You need to cut that out. You gonna make me hurt somebody over you."

"Camer—"

"Sshhh…don't say a word. Let our bodies do the talking. We've said enough for today. I've got some things to show you."

He slid his arms under her buttocks and elevated her. With her back against the wall and her legs interlocked with his, he began passionately kissing her neck and breasts. Her lingerie moistened by the juices flowing from his mouth. It was an insatiable craving that Cameron was determined to quench, right here and right now. His hands moved aimlessly all over her body, over and under her garment. It was like he was exploring her body for the first time. It felt new, exhilarating, but yet surprisingly familiar.

He began moving her further down the hallway and into the bedroom. Raven knew that any superpowers she may have possessed to resist him were nonexistent within the boundaries of the bedroom. In that room, nothing mattered but pleasuring one another. No safe words were needed; they loved each other within a circle of trust. No inhibitions were allowed; they felt restrictions deflated the

energy in the room. Everything was fair game if it meant

the other person would be aroused and feel pleasure. It was

an act of the mind and body causing them to connect

beyond the natural. It felt divine, and spiritual in a sense.

To have Cameron overtaking her body and mind

simultaneously drove her soul to its perimeter making her

want to explode. This was more than sex. It was more than

a fling or raunchy love affair. This man touched the depths

of her soul, and she touched his in ways that no one ever

could. No one other than them would be able to understand

their biological and psychological chemistry.

"Raven, can I ask you a question?"

"Of course, you can," said Raven as she lay on the

bed gleaming from the after-sex glow.

"Can you promise me that you won't ever leave

me?"

"Cameron…seriously?"

"C'mon, Raven. I am serious. Promise me."

She knew she planned to marry Jared whenever he officially proposed but had no idea as to when that would be. But she did not want to give Cameron false hope that she would be entangled in this love bizarre forever. It would be a lie. At some point she wanted out. She wanted to breathe and live an honest life free from the disillusions that haunted her daily.

"I'm here with you in this moment, babe. Let's just enjoy it. No one knows what tomorrow will bring. You may wake up one day and decide that I'm not what you want or need. You may be cured and no longer in need of your medicine, as you call it."

"Never. That will never happen. Each day I wake up and choose you."

She wanted to trust and believe in his words. She knew he was sincere in his own way but could not erase the fact that he was a married man. Although not happily married, he was still very much married to a woman who apparently had no clue how her husband felt.

"What is love to you, Cameron?" questioned Raven.

"You are love, Raven. We are love," Cameron said with conviction.

"But what does that mean? What does that really mean to you? You took vows to be faithful to Monica. How do I know you'd ever be faithful to me?"

"Me and you are not like Monica and me and you know that. There is no comparison. It is just a matter of time before our marriage ends. We rarely talk. We don't have sex. There is nothing there. I don't want to go on much longer pretending to be the husband I am not."

As he rolled over to face Raven, he placed his hand behind the small of her neck. Bringing her in closer, he looked her in her eyes and said, "Raven, you are the one that completes me. I don't want anyone else but you."

Her eyes began to swell with emotion. The feelings in her heart were rising to the surface faster than she could control. She laid there hanging on to every word, with every bit of hope that there was some truth buried in his declaration. She believed he loved her, but the reality was he shouldn't. She couldn't be the one for him if she was the number two. He wiped the tears from her eyes and softly kissed her cheek.

"Everything is going to be fine. It will all work out. I promise. Don't cry."

He continued to hold and comfort her like only he could. Reassuring her from his touch that everything would be as he said. The next morning, she reached over to hit the snooze button on her alarm clock and noticed a jewelry box with a note. She sat up in the bed and opened the note first. It was from Cameron. It read:

"Our love will never end. Forever yours. - Cameron"

It was a Tiffany necklace with two interlocking circles symbolizing a continuous flow of their love. No definitive beginning or end but intertwined and everlasting.

Cameron insisted on driving the girls to the airport for their weekend trip. Brandi met up at Raven's house and they waited for his arrival.

"Your boy is a trip," said Brandi, "I can't believe he is taking us to the airport. He just has to be involved in everything."

"Yea, he wants to see his wife and mistress off. I guess you can't blame him for that," laughed Raven.

"Girrlllll…you two are something else. That is all I am going say. I still can't believe we are going on vacation with his wife. Do you think she has any idea at all about you two?"

"No, I don't think so. You know she called me the other day because Cameron didn't come home for hours after work. She has doubts about him being faithful."

"What? And what did you say?"

"Well, I definitely did not tell her that he was at my house," laughed Raven. "But I told her that if he was cheating then she would know. That she should watch his pattern of behavior and actions and if they change then maybe something is going on."

"How do you do that?"

"Do what?"

"Give advice to a woman whose husband you're sleeping with?"

Raven inhaled and exhaled deeply. "Girl, I don't know. I didn't know what to say or how to react. She caught me off guard. I thought she was calling me about the deposit for the hotel reservations but instead she wanted to discuss Cameron and her suspicions. What the heck was I supposed to say?"

"I don't even know. I guess you handled it as best you could. But don't you find it interesting that she reached out to you?"

"Well, who else would she reach out to? She doesn't really know anyone around here and plus she knows that Cameron and I are close."

"Ha ha! Hell yeah, y'all close. A little too damn close. I bet she don't know just how close, close is with ya'll!"

"You're so silly, Brandi!" exclaimed Raven. "They just pulled up. Get your stuff. Let's go. Don't mention none of this in the car either!"

The ride to the airport was fairly quiet. Just a few niceties exchanged between Cameron and the riders related to the weather, their destination, and traffic. Nothing notable that one would remember after making it through security and boarding the plane. When they arrived at the airport, Cameron helped everyone with their luggage, kissed and hugged both Monica and Raven, and wished everyone a safe trip.

"I'll call you when we arrive, sweetie," said Monica while blowing him a kiss. He did not return the kiss but instead nodded his head, got back in the truck and headed home.

The hotel looked exactly like the online pictures. Modern art deco architecture, red accent pillows in the hotel lobby and the tropical rooftop pool looked like something torn out of a travel magazine. It was breathtaking. Raven could see why so many people and well-known celebrities enjoyed vacationing in South Beach, Miami. From the hotel balcony, small cafes, indie shops and world-renowned restaurants fancied after some of the greatest chefs, lined Ocean Drive giving them a ringside view of all the action.

High-end cars crawled down the street stopping often to admire the bikini-dressed women in all shapes, sizes, and colors. South Beach didn't just have a vibe - it was a vibe. The sun and humidity were practically intolerable though and the girls decided to rest at the hotel until the temperature cooled down a bit. They agreed to meet back up in the lobby at 5:30 pm and head to the beach which was just a short walk from the hotel.

In the hotel room, Raven unpacked her suitcase and put her belongings inside the drawers. On the accent chair she laid out the swimsuit she planned to wear, along with a pair of sandals, beach hat, and shades. She was ready for whatever the night had in store. It felt good to be disconnected from thoughts of Jared and Cameron. She was a strong woman but juggling both men was an exhausting feat at times. There were extreme high's and low's that chipped away at her sanity bit by bit. It would get overwhelming where she found it hard to breathe and even think sometimes. She plopped down on the bed, laid back and outstretched her arms. "Aaahhh, yes. I totally needed this," mumbled Raven to herself. "No work phone, no text messages, no men, no expectations. This is living," she thought.

She didn't realize how tired she was and drifted into a deep sleep almost as soon as her head hit the pillow. The last thing she remembered was laying on the bed listening to the sounds of the cars driving by and distant chatter from the passersby. She was awakened by a knock at the door. It was Brandi. Raven was supposed to meet them in the lobby fifteen minutes ago. She rushed to get dressed and hurried downstairs.

The beach was gorgeous and filled with tons of people. As you looked down the shoreline you could see private cabanas in almost every color and design: red, orange, yellow, blue, green, beige, white, pinstripe. Another postcard perfect scene. They decided to make their mark in an empty space just big enough for the three of them near a few other adults who apparently had been tanning for the past few hours.

Raven laid on her back looking up towards the sun. The warm rays felt good against her skin. She looked around for a moment and noticed several people going topless. She thought to herself, I should try that.

"Hey guys, I think I am going to slip my top off and sunbathe on this beach. Y'all wanna join me?"

"Ha! You're crazy, girl," laughed Brandi. "Naw, I'm good. You have at it," said Brandi.

"Oh, my goodness, Raven! Cameron would kill me if he found out I did that," gasped Monica. "You go ahead though!"

Raven didn't come that far to lay on the beach and be a prude. She reached behind her back and unhooked her top with one hand and untied the string behind her neck with the other. She was a well-endowed woman and as soon as her top came off it was like the levees breaking in New Orleans, everything just poured forward. Monica and Brandi snickered and shook their heads at Raven, but it didn't matter. She was in her power zone and doing what it was she wanted to do for a change.

As she lies there, a man approached her. She thought he was going to comment on her large breast size but instead he knelt down on one knee and began trying to sell her tickets to an elite party hosted by a top deejay later that evening. He went on and on about how live the party would be and the special guest lineup. This felt awkward, she thought. She'd never sat and held a random conversation half naked out in public with a man before. This was different for sure. After he finished his spiel, she declined the offer and thanked him for his time. Back to the sunbathing with no tan lines, she thought.

"Hey, Raven," yelled Monica. "Do you think Cameron is cheating on me?"

"What do you mean?" questioned Raven.

"I mean do you think he is cheating on me? I've been observing his behaviors like you said and something just doesn't feel right. He is so distant these days. I was hoping this trip would be good for us. I thought some time

a part would make him miss me and hopefully bring us

closer together."

"Wow," said Raven. How was she going to respond

to this line of questioning unbiased? She was happy to hear

that he was pulling away from his wife because she could

tell he was drawing nearer to her. But, as a woman, her

heart also cried for Monica who was blatantly torn by the

actions of her husband. A part of her felt that Monica had

the right to know about Cameron's deceitful ways even if it

compromised her relationship with him.

"Well, to be honest, Monica. I do hear things, but I

am not sure how true they are."

"Like what kind of things?"

"Well…," Raven cleared her thought and tried to

muster up the courage to feed her some level of truth to

help pacify her curiosity. "…I mean I hear that he can be

pretty flirtatious with women and sometimes may lead them on. I think he has other female friends besides me, too. But I don't know for certain if he is having sex with any of those women. Have you asked him," Raven questioned as she turned towards Monica with piercing eyes?

"God no! I wouldn't dare ask him, Raven. He'd never tell me the truth anyway. You know how charming and evasive he can be. You can never tell if he is telling the truth."

"You're right. What was I thinking," replied Raven? "So, what are you going to do?"

"I don't know. I love him but I just don't trust him anymore."

An awkward silence traded places with the stench of salt in the air. Both noticeable and heavy. Unsure of what to say next, Brandi and Raven forced a fake smile, shrugged their shoulders, then slipped in their Air Pods and listened to music. Music served as the catalyst that helped Raven transform life perils into peaceful solitude. As a young girl, Raven's grandfather introduced her to music, so it became the foundation for her appreciation of all genres.

Everything grew from music: love, laughter, tears, encouragement, motivation and sometimes rage. She could recall the first cassette tape he gave her. Phoebe Snow was the artist. Phoebe had a bluesy sounding voice that was strong and distinctive. Once you heard her bellow out a ballad you were drawn in never to forget the musical narrative experience. Music was a part of her life as much as food and water. She could not live without it. The lyrical poetry was there supporting her through the tough times and encouraging her through the good times.

The girl's trip to Miami was not long enough. Raven could have used just a few more days of solace away from the noise of life. Honestly, the thought of delving back into life as she left it was causing her some anxiety. She accepted responsibility for the choices that led her to where she was; single and in love with two best friends, but it did not change that she wished for a different life. She craved for a life of simplicity. A life where she was in love with one man – her husband and lived in a big house filled with a few children and a couple of dogs. *Was that too much to wish for?* she often thought. Was she not as deserving of a 'good life' as any other successful woman?

Raven wanted to be loved and experience the fairytale life she read about in children's books. Still, she was starting to think that would never happen because of the choices she was making. As a child, her grandmother always preached, "Be careful what kind of soil you plant your seeds in because you are going to reap whatever it is you sow. Good or bad things will surely come to you so choose wisely child." According to grandma, bad soil produced bad crops so one should never waste their energy planting a righteous seed in a place destined to decay. Maybe grandma was right. Within her words were golden nuggets of wisdom.

These words lingered in Raven's mind forcing her to reflect upon the mistakes she made and was still making. Seeds were definitely being planted but Raven knew that Cameron was 'bad soil'. Their relationship was not fated to blossom because it was built on lies, sex, and deceit. It was exciting at first. Hell, it was downright sexy! It was everything a woman could have imagined. Until the emotions got entangled with the lust. This entanglement created a bond that was unshakeable and everlasting, it seemed.

As Raven sat on the plane waiting for takeoff, she pondered on those golden nuggets of wisdom bestowed on her years ago. She felt like she was standing at a fork in the road and was compelled to immediately decide which path to take. Unsure of where either road would lead, she fretted about which way to choose. She was a woman of logic and understood the facts versus the imagery. She knew for a fact that Cameron would not leave his wife, nor did she want him to leave. She also knew for a fact that although Jared loved her, he was pulling away due to her inability to commit. She was not sure how much longer he would wait for her.

With each passing day he became more and more distant. Although it was a pleasant feeling to imagine herself in love and living happily ever after with Cameron, that image quickly faded when she visualized all of the people who would be hurt by their selfishness: Jared, Monica, family, and close friends. To be with Cameron meant that she could not be with Jared and isolated from anyone within their circle. That feeling did not sit well with her. It made her feel like she would always be missing out on something and constantly doubting the decision she made.

There was no fairness for all in taking that pathway, only sadness and anger; products of seeds planted in bad soil. Her only other option was to take the path that led to a life without either Jared or Cameron. It was hard to even imagine what life would be like without either of them. At first thought, it was frightening and left Raven feeling helplessly lost. But then, after a second thought, she started to feel a strong sense of relief. The weighted feeling she'd carried for many years started to slowly dissipate. Her shoulders began to feel looser; her breathing was less heavy and her mind became clearer. Although it's been said that the heart wants what the heart wants, it was becoming more obvious as to which path to take.

As the plane hurried down the runway preparing to climb towards the clouds, Raven nestled in her seat, closed her eyes and drifted off to sleep. She vowed to herself to have an answer to her own burning question of which path to choose by the time she awoke. She refused to remain in this limbo-love state any longer. It was draining and exhausting to keep up. Some decisions needed to be made and things needed to change. There was a sense of urgency brewing in her veins. She was in pursuit of true happiness and nothing or no one was going to distract her.

There comes a time in everyone's life where they take stock of their life, evaluate where they are versus where they want to be. This was one of those times for Raven. Someone once told her, "If it is to be, then it's up to me!" She bought into this mantra and was prepared to live by it. Sure, her life had not gone as expected, but it was never too late to change the trajectory. The time had come; actually it was long overdue.

After about an hour, Raven made it home from the airport. She could not recall the traffic lights or stop signs they stopped at, nor the streets they turned down. All she remembered was the Uber driver pulling into her driveway leaving the car idling while waiting for her to exit. Her mind was occupied with life changing thoughts which made her unaware of anything else. As she reached to take her suitcase from the trunk, she felt her cell phone vibrate.

"Are you back yet?"

It was Cameron. She glared at her phone for a few moments, then slid it back into her purse. She had no desire to respond or entertain his rhetoric. Her phone vibrated several more times throughout the night and like the first text message, she ignored each one finally deciding to turn her phone off to avoid any more disturbances. Peace reigned supreme in her life right now. For once she could inhale and exhale without any worries or stress. It was an addictive feeling that encapsulated her soul and refused to flee. It was time she started loving herself above all else.

Self-love was a phrase that Raven knew little about. Since she was young she was taught to love and do for others. Sure she knew to always keep her appearance up, take care of herself, and speak well with others, but she wasn't taught how to put her own happiness above others' needs. This was something that she was learning and embracing. When she reflected on the past few years she realized that she spent the majority of her time trying to please everyone else and it was exhausting. She felt compelled to make sure Cameron's needs were met, both physically and emotionally.

She focused on ensuring Jared did not feel the distance between them and that he was still the center of her life. She was always available to her friends and family as a shoulder to cry on or to lend an ear. But who was there for Raven while she was busy pouring into others? Who was there to inspire her when her world crashed and she felt the desperate need to exhale? No one, that's who. The more she pondered, the more she realized that she needed to start being more selfish with her time and energy. Being less accessible to her lovers and spending time getting to know herself was becoming her main priority. She had reached a point where she craved more from life and for herself. Confucius once said, 'He who conquers himself is the mightiest warrior''. Raven was determined to conquer whatever was holding her back from a fulfilling and honest life, even if it meant walking away from everything and everyone she knew.

Days passed by and Raven continued to ignore voicemail and text messages from Cameron and Jared. There was a growing concern with each message left. What started as a 'just checking in on you' message quickly turned to 'do I need to call the police to see if you are still alive'? She wasn't sure how much longer she could keep them both at bay and even thought about changing her phone number. Part of her glowed inside by their affirmations of concern but the other part of her was frustrated by what her life had become. She knew better but fell victim to her own selfish desires. She wanted the best of both worlds until those worlds secretly collided. She was

trying to move away from the chaos of a love triangle and

could not understand why Cameron did not understand her

need for peace and Jared her need for space.

Later that night, Raven relaxed on the couch sipping

her favorite red wine when she heard a loud knock at her

front door. It was almost 10:00 pm and she knew it could

only be one person. The lights were out inside her home

and her car was parked in the garage out of sight. She was

hoping to give the appearance that no one was home. She

did not make a move to answer the door, instead she

continued sipping her liquid solitude. After a few minutes,

the knocking stopped. She exhaled a sigh of relief and

started making her way upstairs towards her bedroom.

As she crossed past the foyer, she saw someone

peeking in the window. A voice shouted out, "I know you

are in there, Raven! I can see you! Let me in!!" Was

Cameron seriously peeping through her window watching

her shadows move throughout the house? A few seconds later, the knocking resumed at the front door, growing louder and more forceful.

Dammit! Why can't he just leave me alone and go back to his wife? she thought. Grudgingly she decided to open the door and let him in. She knew he was persistent and would continue to stalk her until he got the answers he needed. Dressed in her traditional long, silk night gown she opened the door. "Hello, Cameron." He quickly pushed past her and made his way in rambling as he walked towards the living room. "Why haven't you answered my calls and text messages? What is wrong with you?"

"I've just needed a break from life and from you."

"What the hell are you talking about? I haven't done anything to you. Why are you being so damn selfish?" yelled Cameron with a bit of fire in his eyes.

"Well, maybe it is about time I be a little selfish don't ya think?" Raven said sarcastically. "For years, I've allowed you to selfishly use me at your disposal. I'm tired of it, Cameron. This has to stop." He looked around the house as if he was searching for someone.

"You got some dude over here, Raven? Is that what this is all about? You trying to leave me for some other dude?" It was clear his ego could not grasp the thought of Raven wanting to move on simply because she had had enough.

"No, Cameron. I am not seeing anyone else. I've just been doing me these days so you can stop with your police search."

He huffed and puffed for a few seconds while pacing back and forth in the hallway. "She put me out."

"What are you talking about? Who put you out?"

"Monica! The bitch put me out," exclaimed Cameron.

"And why would she do that, Cameron?"

"I don't know. You tell me! She came back from that girls trip y'all had and started acting a damn fool. I knew that was a bad idea."

"I don't know what you are talking about. Nothing happened on that trip except us having a good time."

"Oh, so you didn't tell her that I was cheating on her with a bunch of chics?"

Raven's eyes grew larger and a lump formed in her throat. Did Monica actually go back and tell Cameron some things she'd said. Unbelievable, she thought. Then again, it was her husband and she had every right to confront him with whatever was on her mind.

"Well…I may have said something about that."

"Why in the hell would you do that?" yelled Cameron. "So, you were trying to get me put out? Is that what this shit is about? You know damn well I cannot come live with you so what the hell were you thinking?" He stood with his eyes fixed on hers demanding answers. He wanted answers she could not give. She had no idea why she said those things to Monica and never even thought through her words' repercussions. She just knew in that moment on the beach she felt sorry for Monica. In a twisted way she actually thought she was helping her by easing her doubts. But as Cameron stood before her now enraged and desperate for understanding, she realized she made a poor decision that day about telling her anything.

"Look Cameron. I am sorry about what I said but you cannot deny that it is true."

"Raven, it doesn't matter if it's true. You betrayed me! I would never have done that to you! I would never tell Jared about us. Why would you do this?" He buried his face in the palms of his hands and sobbed. Raven had never seen Cameron so unglued. He always portrayed himself as this strong brute who could take any blow that came his way. But in this moment he was weakened. With every accusation he spoke she became more and more remorseful.

"Cameron, I am sorry. I did not mean for this to happen. Please forgive me." As those words left her mouth she thought to herself, how did he just become the victim? What was she saying? He created this madness with his constant pursuit of her. She was feeling so conflicted. She knew that even though she shouldn't, she loved this man and regardless of their chaotic life she did not want to see him in pain. She had to somehow make this right. As wrong as right could be, she walked towards him and took him in her arms. To feel his touch again brought back a rush of memories. In this moment, she felt safe and whole again. Reuniting with his body was making her melt inside.

No matter how hard she tried to resist him, she fell victim every time. Their connection was strong and unshakeable, and she hated the power he had over her.

"Cameron, why don't you stay here for the night? We can talk about things in the morning."

"Okay...okay. Thank you," he said in between his emotional cry for help.

"Everything will be fine. I promise," she whispered in his ear, but unsure of her own words. She did not know how to rebound from this because she could not take back what she said to Monica and she also could not go into any details and reveal that she was the one he spent his time with when he was not at home. All of her peaceful days ended right here. His visit teleported her right back to the place she did not want to be – the love triangle.

With his head hung low, Cameron made his way upstairs towards the bedroom. He slipped off his clothes and climbed into bed waiting for Raven to join him. Raven needed just a moment to gather her thoughts and emotions so she retreated to the bathroom. She needed to take a hard look at herself in the mirror to question what she was doing and what she was about to do. She felt like an alcoholic that had been sober for days and was now about to fall back off the wagon. She knew how this night would go and to be honest it was starting to go exactly how she wanted it to go. She wanted to feel him inside of her again. She wanted to lay her head in the crease of his arm, her safe place, and feel their souls touch. She needed this right now more than anything.

Calm and collected she exited the bathroom and made her way to the bed. Slowly pulling back the covers, she mounted him.

"What are you doing?" Placing her finger across his soft lips she said, "Sshhh, don't talk. You've said enough for one night."

She reached between his thighs and began to moan. While throwing her head back and slightly arching her body backwards, she guided him inside of her. Oh, how good it felt to feel him again, she thought. She gently rocked back and forth and then in a circular motion. With every grinding movement, she moaned louder and louder. Passion filled every crevice of the room. He loved it. He loved her and she loved him. His hands were firmly rested around the small of her waist giving him leverage to thrust her towards him even more. After a few minutes of symphonic lovemaking, he moved her off of him and onto her stomach. He yearned to take her from behind submissively. Tenderly pulling her hair and uttering sexual banter while penetrating her brought him the greatest pleasure.

"Raven, I love you baby…I don't want to ever be without you…I need you."

"I know…I know…don't stop."

Monique DeMille   Mosaic Anthology

The headboard knocked against the wall uncontrollably. Raven reached her hand up to hold on and brace herself. As the headboard knocking subsided, a distant knock was heard from downstairs.

"Are you expecting someone?"

"No, I wasn't even expecting you for that matter," laughed Raven.

Raven quickly grabbed her robe and flew downstairs to check on the noise coming from the unexpected visitor at her front door. She could see a shadow through the side windowpane as she approached the door. As she drew closer and reached to turn the light on she gasped. She couldn't believe what her eyes were revealing to her mind. Jared was on her front porch staring her right into her eyes through the windowpane. Her knees were weak and her palms were sweaty. She could not explain why Cameron was upstairs in her bed. She knew with certainty that the

120

two worlds of her love triangle had just collided never to remain separated again from this point forward.

Shakingly she reached to unlock the door and turned the knob. She couldn't think of one excuse to use that would explain why Cameron was at her house.

"Jared? What are you doing here?"

"What am I doing here? Are you serious," questioned Jared with a firm tone? "I don't know, Raven. Maybe it has something to do with the fact that you have not answered any of my calls or text messages in days. I was beginning to worry."

"Well, there is no need to worry. I am fine."

"Oh, I can see that you are fine. But what I want to know now is why the hell Cameron's truck is parked in your driveway!"

"Look Jared, I-I-". He firmly grabbed her arm, stared her in the eyes and awaited an answer.

"Don't even think about lying to me, Raven!"

A million thoughts were racing frantically through her mind but not one logical lie was able to find its way out. This was the moment she always dreaded. The moment when the gig was up. When Jared caught her in an unexplainable position with Cameron that would lead her to do nothing other than tell the truth.

"He stopped by because Monica threw him out and he had nowhere else to go." There, she thought, that was a truthful statement. She was not lying. Had Monica not thrown him out then he probably would not have come by her house that night. Instead he would have continued to text and call a little while longer, she hoped.

"And why did Monica put his ass out?" questioned Jared.

"She thought he was cheating on her."

"With who? You?"

"What are you talking about, Jared? Why would she think he was cheating with me?" probed Raven. She was trying to figure out just how much Jared suspected the two of them were having an affair but wasn't sure he'd take the bait.

"You know why. You two have always been closer than you should have been."

"I don't know what you're talking about. I was -..."

They were interrupted by Cameron making his way down the stairs wearing only his jeans and no shirt. This is about to get bad real fast, Raven thought.

"What are you doing over here, Bruh?"

"Aaahh, don't come over here with all of that nonsense, Jared. It's too late for that shit," said Cameron.

"You fucking my girl?"

"And what if I am? I guess that would mean she wasn't really your girl, huh?"

Raven could not believe Cameron said what he just said. He was not making the situation any better with his pompous attitude. Over the years she had grown to appreciate his cockiness and strong will. She found it enhanced his sex appeal and bedroom performance but now was definitely not the time to be ornery. Jared was here and was clearly pissed off. All Raven wanted to do was try to diffuse the situation.

"What did you say to me?"

"You heard me. Newsflash for you, Bruh. She's not your girl."

Jared charged across the foyer in lightning speed. Grabbing Cameron by the neck, Jared threw him against the wall. Blows were exchanged and Raven stepped out of the way to avoid having one land on her.

"Stop it! Stop it!" Raven yelled. "This is crazy!"

The two rumbled on the floor like uncaged lions fighting for survival. Venom seethed through Jared's teeth with each blow while Cameron spewed visceral remarks about Jared being a pathetic and weak man.

"You ain't shit, Dude. That's all you got?" said Cameron. Cameron managed to pin Jared down on his back. The tension was rising in the room and Raven had no idea how to stop it.

"Stop it! Cameron get off of him! You're going to hurt him! Please stop!" The punches back and forth continued until Jared was able to break free of Cameron's hold. It seemed as though the brawl was coming to an end.

"I thought we were boys! And you been over here fucking my girl this whole time?" The more Jared thought about the two of them spending time together behind his back the angrier he became. He charged at Cameron again with a blow, but this time he missed and punched a hole in the wall instead. Cameron picked up a nearby statue and attempted to hit Jared but missed causing it to shatter into pieces on the floor. Everything was spiraling out of control.

"I am going to call the police if you two grown ass men don't stop it right now!"

The energy in the room began to ease as the two men stood winded against opposite walls of the room staring each other down. The visible hatred between the two men was thick in the air making it hard to breathe and think about what to do next. The evening had turned out to be nothing like Raven expected. What started as a night of rekindling with her secret lover had turned out to be a bloody dual between two friends in love with the same woman.

"I cannot deal with you or any of this, Raven. I can't fucking believe you. My best friend? Really?"

pleaded Jared. Cameron just stood there speechless. For the first time that Raven could recall Cameron had absolutely nothing to say. No manly remarks. No apologies. Only shame filled his battered face.

"I do not want to hear from either of you ever again. Lose my number and forget you ever knew me. I'm done," proclaimed Jared. "I am done." He shook his head at the both of them, turned away and walked out the door. Raven knew she would never hear from him again. Too much had happened to go back to the way things were and too much had happened to move things forward. It was finally over. The love triangle was finally over, and she could breathe freely.

"I think you should leave too. I never want to see you again either, Cameron."

Without uttering a word, Cameron grabbed his things from upstairs and left. Raven closed and locked the door behind him. The reality of never seeing either of them again set in. Falling to her knees she cried uncontrollably. This was not how things were supposed to end, she thought. She was not supposed to lose them both. This was not fair. She wanted her happy ending. She wanted her dream of a faithful husband, big house, children and a good life and not the nightmare she just experienced.

She sat on the floor staring at the broken pieces left behind. It was in this moment she felt the symbolism of her life. The pile of porcelain represented the mess she had made. All of her bad decisions, hurt, pain, frustration and bad seeds laid buried in that pile. It was time to put the pieces of her life back together. She needed to start planting seeds into good soil so she could reap the desires of her heart.

Months had passed since that dreadful night but Raven thought of it often. Never acting on any impulses to contact Jared or Cameron, she pushed through each day focused on becoming a better version of herself. In time, she thought, they would each become a distant memory. A season of her past never to be visited again. Brandi tried to convince her to join a dating app to find a boyfriend, but Raven had no interest. She felt it was still too soon to date and did not want the headache or any more heartache. She was in a much better place these days. She was enjoying the simple pleasure of life like jogging, strolls in the park, reading books, and taking in movies from time to time. Life was now simple and not complicated. There were no more late-night visits from Cameron. No more sneaking around and lying. It felt good to live an honest and stress-free life.

Raven stopped by a Thai restaurant on the way home from work. It was one of her favorite spots she frequented. While standing in line to place her order she noticed the man in front of her constantly looking back in her direction. So, she turned and looked towards the door to see where his eyes led. There was no one there. *What was he looking at?* she wondered

The next time he turned around he smiled directly at her. *I think this man is checking me out,* she thought. After placing his order and paying the cashier he stepped aside and sat alongside the wall in one of the red chairs. The order taker knew her well and repeated her usual order aloud to her. She confirmed and reached in her purse to pull out her wallet. The cashier immediately said, "No payment for you. The man in front of you already paid for your order."

"He did? Are you serious?"

"Yes, ma'am. Take a seat and your order will be ready in about twenty minutes."

"Ohh…well…thank you," Raven was speechless. She could not understand why this stranger would do that. Maybe it was one of those fads like she heard on the radio where the person in front of you generously pays for your order hoping you will pay the gesture forward. She wasn't sure but felt compelled to approach him and thank him for the kind gesture.

"Hello. That was very kind of you. Thank you so much."

"It was my pleasure. If you do not mind me asking, what is your name?"

"No, I do not mind. My name is Raven. And yours?"

"Nice to meet you, Raven. That is such a beautiful name and very fitting. My name is John. It is a pleasure to meet you."

"Can I ask you a question?"

"Sure, shoot."

"Why did you buy me dinner?"

"Well, as I stood in line I could not help but be struck by your beauty. I wanted to ask you out to dinner but couldn't figure out the best way to do it. So, I figured I'd buy you dinner and then ask you to join me. Kind of silly, huh," he said with a chuckle.

"Ha! Not silly at all. I am speechless. No one has ever done this kind of thing before."

"Well, I do not know why not. You are simply gorgeous. So, will you have dinner with me?"

"Yes, John, I will. And it is so nice to meet you as well."

Raven was taken aback by this stranger's kind gesture. He was extremely attractive, had a pleasant smile, a muscular physique and was polite but he was not her usual type. She always dated black men and this man was white. Tall, handsome, and white. He picked out a table near the far east corner of the room. He pulled her chair out and invited her to sit down. *Wow, and he is chivalrous too,* she thought.

There must be something wrong with him. He was probably emotionally messed up from a previous divorce or girlfriend or the stalker type. They sat in the restaurant talking for hours. She was intrigued by his conversation. He spoke about his family, where he grew up, his career, travels, and hobbies. He was so unlike 'the others' she'd dated in the past. Everything about him was refreshing and flowed easily. As the evening came to a close, he asked if he could see her again.

"Yes, I think I'd like that, John. Here's my number."

"Thanks for a lovely evening, Raven. I really enjoyed our conversation and connection. Here I thought I was only stopping by this place to pick up some Thai takeout but instead I was fortunate enough to spend the evening with the most beautiful woman in town. I look forward to seeing you again real soon." He walked her out to her car and opened the door for her to get in. Raven was filled with excitement and wonderment on the drive home. She was eager to hear from John again and, like him, was looking forward to their first official date. As she pulled into her driveway she saw her phone illuminate with a text message from John.

"Thanks again. This is my number. Hope you made it home safely. See you soon."

To be continued...

A Monologue

Intrusive thoughts linger

Like stale cigarette smoke in an empty room

Hope opens the door and waits patiently with Joy

But the aroma stays caged

Undeceived but aware

It stands still

Afraid to creep forward

It regresses

It smothers me

Lingering long past its time

Winding down deeper

Deeper

Retreating to familiar crevices mustering up more strength

Oh, to be free from my mind

To part from the grim realities

And ravel with my fantasies

But it lingers on, long past its time

Untitled

My smile is forced

My pain is brute

My sarcasm is a subtle cry

The laughter you hear is mocked

The disappointments are genuine

The tears I shed are but always in solitude

In the center of the storm, I stand

In the midst of the hurt, I survive

Deep in the trenches, I evolve and come alive

Within myself I find a trusted ally

At the end of the beginning to an end, I am unwavering

The Rain

Things are not always what they seem, and beauty can be found in the most obscure places. On a rainy, dreary day far from the blaring sounds of city life, three small children are playing near an abandoned warehouse. They are running amok wearing only shirts, no shoes, no shorts. Splashing and laughing as they leap in and out of the murky puddles. They are naive to the potential dangers that exist in the trash field water nearby. For not even a mile away is a penitentiary that houses criminals.

Signs sit along the highway to alert motorist to refrain from picking up any hitchhikers because they could be escapees from the nearby facility. The children are much too young to interpret and heed the warning signs. For the children, life is good. Embracing the rain and all of the friendly creatures and joys it brings. They enjoy everything from the worms to the beetles to the mudslides, oblivious to anything or anyone outside their circle of fun, including the

broken man piercing in the distance from the barred

window. The man was once childlike and carefree, but now

older and confined, he sits alone with his thoughts. Seeing

the adventurous children outside triggered bittersweet

memories of Declan's childhood.

As a child he spent most of his days with his

grandparents causing him to be wise beyond his years. His

mother, Gina, was a seamstress who worked long hours at a

small shop in the impoverished side of town. Her face,

although soft and supple, bore signs of stress and

exhaustion for a woman her age. Her hands were worn and

arched beyond straightening from the repetitious

movements. On most days, she would work up to eighteen

hours with only a few quick breaks in between. Just long

enough to eat a small meal fit for the poorest of paupers.

In an overly crowded room, the ladies were

expected to work almost nonstop. A bucket was left in the

corner of the room for each to use to expel themselves. It was changed out every two hours or so causing an unbearable smell and intolerable working conditions. As a single parent, Gina knew that she needed the job because her family depended on it. Work with decent pay was scarce, so she pushed through each shift without complaining. Showing gratitude to her employer daily by using please's and thank you's and staying to work however long they required. Accustom to Gina's absence from the home, her parents took on the responsibility of caring for Declan.

Declan's grandfather, Richard, was a war veteran. Injured during battle and unable to find work, he spent his days either in the back room asleep or sitting on the front porch gazing at the sky mumbling to himself. Declan would sometimes see Richard out on the porch and be curious as to what he was doing. One night he decided to venture outside and ask.

"What are you looking at, Papa," a young Declan asked hoping to gain insight into his grandfather's world.

"I hope you never see what I don't see," replied Richard.

"What's that, Papa? The stars and clouds above?"

"No, son. The future that will never come for me. A future interrupted and forgotten," replied Richard in a somber tone. "Don't let your dreams flee you faster than a cheetah can run," said Richard. "Don't you do it. Promise me."

"I promise, Papa. I promise," said Declan not really understanding the commitment he just made to the man he admired. Nor prepared to even begin to know how to live up to the vow he just made. Perplexed with his own words, Declan sat in silence with his Papa looking up at the speckled sky.

Declan was not old enough to understand life's perils or his grandfather's abstract emotions. All he understood was how full of life he was when he was able to help his grandma, Emma, in the field. Their day would begin shortly before the sun peeked over the hills. The smell of pork sizzling and buttermilk biscuits in the oven was enough to awaken him from a deep sleep. The aroma was so tantalizing that even the neighborhood dogs perked up and waited at the door for the morning scraps to be served. Declan would dash to grab his britches and shirt from the edge of his bed and head straight to the kitchen. Once he made it, he would run up behind his grandmother, wrapping his arms around the small of her waist, and give her a big hug.

"Guess who," said Declan. She would burst into a hearty laughter. She enjoyed the guessing game just as much as he did. Each time leading the banter with a different animal.

"Gee, I don't know. Could it be a bear that's wrapped around me so tight?"

"No, I am not a bear. Guess again."

"Hmmmm, could it be a possum? I know how much they love to cuddle up next to people just before daybreak."

"No, Grandma I am not a possum either. Guess again," said Declan.

"Hmmm, this is pretty tough! Let's see. Could it be a Siamese cat? Those blue-eyed, furry friends love to give big, warm hugs," said Grandma.

"No, Grandma. It's me! It's me, Declan!"

"Ohh, I had no idea it was you, Declan! You had me fooled," said Grandma.

Looking back, out in the fields is where Declan learned his life lessons. In between harvesting potatoes, Grandma took pride in explaining how a young man should behave in the world, how to earn an honest living and why having a good education was so important. "Plenty of water and sunshine," his Grandma would say, "is the recipe for the making of a great man - as well as a potato!" It was in these fields and during these times that he began to grow like the harvest around him. He was now a man by age but not necessarily based on the choices he'd made in life.

The rain tapping on the window outside was a constant reminder of Declan's past. As he watched the children explore their surroundings, he reflected upon his childhood years. While most were good but distant memories, others were unforgettable. Those years were when life was much simpler and composed of less options. Options made life complicated. Options meant that you had to choose between one desire and another. The choice always left you feeling deprived of something that could have been but never was. Life, he realized, was unfair and full of sacrifices. All the water and sunshine in the world could not change his current circumstances. He was where

he was because of the sacrifices he made for a different life.

Declan now sits in a small room with an opening

that is approximately forty-two inches tall and four inches

wide. Just large enough for him to see a few feet passed the

wire fence, and the children playing, while catching a

glimpse of occasional sunlight. Throughout the day, and

sometimes late into the night, Declan would spend time

thinking about his mom and Grandma Emma. They always

inspired him with their wisdom and outlook on life. It was

his grandma though who was his number one fan. He could

always depend on her for encouragement through the

toughest times.

He would lie in bed replaying the events of that day,

wishing he could somehow change the outcome.

Unfortunately, life was not a video game that gave you

options for alternate endings. In the real world, actions

were often irrevocable. There was no fairy Godmother

dressed in a ballroom gown, holding a wand waiting to grant you three more chances to get it right. No, in the real world, one immediately became the product of his poor decisions. No rewinds or do-over's allowed. Game over.

Growing up, Sunday dinners were a long-time family tradition. It was a time for everyone to come together and enjoy each other's company. On this particular Sunday, Richard offered to drive to the store and pick up the last-minute grocery items needed for dinner. Gina insisted on going to the store instead and alone. She was so grateful for her parent's help with Declan and wanted to ease their load by handling even the smallest of tasks. Unfortunately, she never made it to the store. As she pulled out of the driveway, she saw her son in the living room window waving and blowing kisses to her.

She quickly returned the gesture but neglected to keep her foot on the brake. At the same time, a truck was barreling down the street. As she rolled directly into its path, it plowed into the car killing her instantly. A young

Declan saw and felt every moment. The rain pouring down

endlessly. The car easing its way down the driveway. He

saw the love in his mother's eyes as she blew kisses back to

him. He felt the impact of the truck as it plowed into his

mother's car. He felt his heart sink, his body go numb and

the tears roll down his face. The rain always brought back

the dormant pain that he tried so hard to forget. Damn the

rain, he thought.

So many questions raced through his mind about

that day. What if my mom never went to the store that day,

would Papa had died instead? Was it my fault she died

because I was distracting her with my airborne kisses? If I

had rode with her would I have died too? Maybe death with

my mother would have been better than life without her, he

thought. Never able to reach a conclusion that would bring

him peace or closure, the thoughts continued to soar, and

the anxieties continued to rise. But he was not alone with

his sorrow. His Grandma and Papa struggled to cope with his mother's death too. Though many days and weeks had passed, the feelings of disbelief and guilt were ever present.

A few months after the fatal accident, Emma was in the kitchen preparing Sunday dinner. Her and Declan arrived home about an hour beforehand after hearing Pastor Ellsworth's message on faith. He spoke about the need for Christians to not only have faith in God but also the need to believe in the supernatural. Declan could not understand how people struggled to believe in the supernatural when people like Superman, Batman and The Flash were performing supernatural acts of courage and kindness every day. The sentiment of the naysayers was beyond his youthful comprehension.

Emma declined Declan's invitation to assist her with preparing the meal that day. Instead she asked that he set the table before his grandfather reached home. Emma taught him long ago the proper way to set a table: two forks to the left of the dinner plate, two spoons and knife to the right with the sharp side of the knife closest to the plate, and the water glass just above the knife. Although she instructed him to place the cloth napkins on the left-hand side, he enjoyed crafting the cloth into different shapes and placing them in the center of the plate, a handsome bowtie, four-leaf clover, or even a swan. He felt it gave the place setting personality.

Just as Declan was finishing the last napkin, Richard stumbled through the door reeking of vodka, cigarette smoke, and salted bar nuts. It was an unpleasant but familiar scent that they had grown accustomed to smelling. For Emma, the extent of her loss from the crash went beyond Gina; she lost her husband on that day, too. Richard had not always been a heavy drinker. He was more of a celebratory drinker where he indulged during holiday's or special events. He started drinking obsessively soon after

Gina's death. He struggled to come to terms with the loss of his only child and said the liquor eased the pain.

Too proud to accept counseling from their pastor or the local VA, he continued to sulk. But he knew the pain was deeper and bigger than anything he had ever experienced. Years of military training prepared him for a different type of battle: man versus man, not man versus self. This was an unfamiliar pain that had no place to go but deeper and deeper. There was no pill he could take that was strong enough and only so much liquor he could consume to mask the emptiness he constantly felt. Times were not always this dreary though. Emma and Richard were elated when they received the news that she was pregnant twenty-seven years ago. They'd tried for years to conceive but to no avail. After three miscarriages and one stillbirth, Gina was born. His world was forever changed by her birth and, in retrospect, her untimely death. Death has a way of either bringing people closer together or further apart.

As Richard made his way towards the couch he rambled about Mr. Harris, the next-door neighbor, and how lucky he was since his wife recently died. Her death granted him the freedom to live, he said. He wished that Emma would hurry up and die so that he could receive a big life insurance payment like Mr. Harris and finally start living the life he always wanted. The time had finally come for his dreams to start manifesting. He was long overdue, he said. As he saw it, he was no longer a father and rightfully did not have to make any more sacrifices for anyone else's happiness except for his own.

His imaginary soap box provided him the platform to spew his, now almost daily, speech of the sacrifices he made for everyone else to live comfortably. Within minutes the rhetoric stopped, and he was fast to sleep. There was peace in the house again, even if only temporarily. Life transformed him and not in a good way. He appeared hardened and angry beyond regression. Emma and Declan could tolerate the stench but not the vulgarities that accompanied it.

Richard was sprawled on the couch when he heard the call that dinner was ready. He jumped up and made his way to the kitchen table in a rage because the sound of Emma's voice startled him from his drunken slumber. He began yelling and cursing about how much he despised her, blaming her for Gina's death. According to him, had she not forgotten to pick up the groceries she needed that day, then his daughter would still be alive. His life, and Declan's, would not have been destroyed. These words cut like a knife through Emma. For months she carried their daughter in her womb not knowing if she would lose her like the others. Now she carried the grief that her daughter was gone forever, never to return.

The malicious epithets eventually turned physical with Richard later grabbing his gun. A gun. The gun. The same gun Richard and Declan used when he was a kid. On any given weekend, the two of them could be found high in the hills hunting deer and sometimes goats. But on this somber evening, an animal was not the target. Grandma Emma was the target, both verbally and physically. Without malevolent intent, Emma pleaded with Richard to calm down. Apologizing for no other reason than to defuse the intensity of the room. She grudgingly accepted blame for Gina's accident to appease him.

As Declan paced back and forth in his cell, his mind instinctively flashed back to that night in the kitchen. He could still remember the aroma of roasted herb chicken, mashed potatoes and gravy, sweet corn on the cob and Grandma's buttermilk biscuits. The faint sound of the television humming in the distance. The stench of his grandfather's drunkenness. The feeling of wanting desperately to save his grandmother from any harm. The gun. The raging thunders. The rain outside. Blaring screams emitting from inside the walls of his childhood home. The sound of cars racing by the house and the

passengers not knowing that just a few feet away stood a

child between a wife and her husband with a loaded gun in

his hand. All the things that caused his heart to ache and his

mind to replay repeatedly.

Declan rushed over to his grandfather and tried to

grab him by the waist. He was small in stature and was

easily brushed aside with one swoop of Richard's hand. He

slid across the floor hitting the wall. With a bit of wind

knocked out of him, Declan managed to get back on his

feet. Grabbing a knife from the kitchen drawer, he charged

back towards Richard. This time will be different, he

thought. He was determined to get the gun out of his Papa's

hand and save his grandmother. Her safety was all that

mattered. The knife pierced Richard's thigh and blood

began pouring out of the wound. Richard continued

aggressively wrestling with Emma but found it hard to keep

his balance with the pain radiating from his leg and the

slipperiness of the tile flooring soaked with his blood. If he could just get him to stop, thought Declan, then all of this could be over.

Why would he want to hurt Grandma when none of this was her fault? He was the one distracting his mother in the window that day. He was the one whom everyone should blame, he thought. Declan looked around the kitchen to see what he could use to end this. He noticed a picture hanging on the wall. He reached for it, turned it around and removed the hanging wire. He quickly ran over to his Papa and looped the wire around his neck, pulling it as tight as his strength allowed. Already barely able to keep his bearing, Richard started falling backward. As he lost his balance the gun released the power that had been caged in all night. A shrill scream rang through the room. It was Grandma. She'd been shot and was lying on the floor gasping for air.

"Noooooo! Graaannndddma! No!" yelled Declan. "What have you done?" He released the wire from Richard's neck and hurried over towards her. He slowly lifted her head and placed it on his lap.

"Declan, I am so sorry it has to end this way," whimpered Emma. "You are such a sweet boy. I love you."

"Ssshhh, don't talk, Grandma. I am going to get you some help. You're gonna be fine," cried Declan. As hard as he tried, he could not muster up enough strength to hold back the tears. The pressure he was applying to her wound was not working. In her eyes and by the blood forming in her mouth, he could see that she was slowly slipping away from him. The only presence of life in the room was the rain pouring down outside. Even the strongest of storms could not wash away the pain he felt from all the death he'd endured. The rain was not his friend but had become his enemy.

Strange Beauty

A caterpillar sheds its skin and flies

A moth flirts with flames ushering in its demise

A chameleon changes it colors and survives

A cereus cactus blooms but one night luring a graceful surprise

Beauty lies not just in the transformation of things

But the expiration of all things

www.ingramcontent.com/pod-product-compliance
Lightning Source LLC
Chambersburg PA
CBHW030345180626
46812CB00007B/2766